Published in the United States by Elij Bryce Publications.

For more information or to contact the author, send correspondence to:

Facebook: Author Malik D. Wilson
Instagram: @Malik_D_Wilson
Email: MalikDWilson22@gmail.com

COVER

Trevion Visuals

Instagram: @TrevionVisuals

• DEDICATED TO •

+ MY KIDS +

Christopher Walters

Jakaii Wilson

Bryonna Saint-Juste

Marlyn Walters

Elijah Wilson

Alyssa Saint-Juste

+ MY COUSINS +

Narik {S.O.} Wilson

Rajohn {1090} Wilson

Emil {DiddyBop} Rutledge

Duquee {Du Ru} Simmons

Elij Bryce Publications & Block-Men Entertainment

Colossal

tha good & tha bad

by:

Tweek SOB

Tuesday April 11th, 2018

8:18 p.m.

16th Street

■ Newark, New Jersey ■

Both Chämp and Phenöm ran to the back of the yard and hopped the back fence. The back fence was the only thing separating 15th Street from 16th Street. They scanned the whole backyard before making a move towards the house 16th Street. The duo knew that somebody could've been back there. Phenöm led the way with both of his guns aimed high. Oh how he was ready to put a bullet in any and everything that stood in their way. Chämp's heart was racing a mile a minute as they neared the back door. They pressed their bodies against the house and Chämp took a deep breath. Chämp looked up to the bathroom window which Doug had left unlocked before they got there. She had left a ladder right underneath the window for them to climb up on. These were the exact plans that Jünior had mapped out for them. Doug just happened to follow every detail down to the very last scribble.

Phenöm started up the ladder first, skipping every other step as he was so anxious to get up in the apartment. Phenöm literally lived for this type of shit! Chämp was hot on Phenöm's trail, promising himself that if he made it out of this alive, he was never again doing no shit like this! As Phenöm neared the window he'd heard one of the dudes walk into the bathroom and close the door. Chämp ran right into Phenöm because he had to stop right where he was at. Phenöm was right at the tip of the window seal peeking into the bathroom, looking right at the dude's back. The dude stood there releasing his bladder which was full of Coronas.

Phenöm wanted to shoot the kid in the back of his head right then and there. However, Phenöm knew that that wasn't a part of the plan at that moment, so he had to wait. To an excited and anxious Phenöm it felt like the kid was pissing for hours. It took him 2 minutes to piss, it was like this nigga had the bladder of a racehorse! Without washing his hands the kid walked back into the living room, leaving the door halfway open instead of closing it back the way it was. Phenöm and Chämp crept into the bathroom having to be extremely careful. They crept towards the door to see how the dudes were positioned within the living room. Everybody were sitting in the living room with their backs towards the bathroom. They were watching the fiendishly amazing Paradice Charms getting fucked on the porno, *Let Off In Me*. Doug was the only female in the room and she was sitting front and center.

She stood there with nothing but her thong and bra on looking like something to eat! She had held the dudes off for as long as she could, but the movie was painting all kinds of pictures for them. Lined up against the wall near the front door was 4 nice size totes right where Doug said they'd be, she had come through for Jünior once again. It was definitely hard to keep these dudes off of her because they'd been trying to get with her since she started working there six months ago, because Doug was bad!

"Come here, Cassey, help me massage this tension between my legs." the dude that had just left the bathroom said, as Phenöm slowly moved towards them.

"Nah, I want her to tell me how many licks it's goin take to get to the center of this tootsie roll pop!" the dude to Doug's left said, openly stroking his dick for all to see.

"Why don't I masturbate this desert eagle to the sweet sound of y'all screaming for mercy!?" Phenöm jumped in, obviously disgusted at how they spoke to Doug.

"Huh!" one dude gasped, quickly turning around to see Phenöm and Chämp standing there.

"What the fuck!" the kid with his dick in his hand replied.

"Nigga, do you know who shit you're fucking wi ---" the last kid began, before Phenöm found salvation within both of his trigger fingers.

BOK, BOK, POP, BOK, POP, BOK.....POP, POP..........BOK !!!

"About fuckin' time!" Doug spat, as she quickly grabbed her clothes and started putting on her blue True Religion jeans, not at all fazed by the scene before her. "Another minute and I was undoubtedly about to be raped in this bitch!"

"I don't know, you might've actually like it." Phenöm returned, standing there in the thick of gun smoke and debris lusting over Doug's body, holding his guns at his side.

"Damn!" Chämp mumbled, seeing Doug's curves for the first time and finding himself getting an erection.

"Fuck you, Phenöm."

"Ummm, can....we get.....the fuck outta here?" Chämp asked, trying to keep his eyes off of Doug, and keep from throwing up at the same time.

Pulling her blue True Religion shirt over her head as quickly as she could, Doug said, "Yes, lets.

While Doug was getting dressed, Phenöm ran into the back room and went straight for the closet. There he found a bookbag filled with drugs and another bookbag filled with cash. He opened them up to check the contents. Seeing what they came for, Phenöm zipped both bags back up and left the room. When he stepped into the living room he saw Chämp handing Doug another bookbag. His eyes lit up when he saw yet another bookbag, thinking that it had more drugs in it.

"Come on, let's get the fuck outta here." Chämp hissed, as he started to get a funny feeling in his stomach.

"I could not agree with you more." Doug joined in, tossing the bookbag onto her back as she made her way towards the back door.

Phenöm pulled his phone out and called Troy to tell her that they were coming out. Troy answered the phone on the first ring, "Yo?"

"We coming out, pull up." Phenöm returned, walking out of the door leaving it wide open.

"That shit was crazy." Doug said, walking down the back hallway steps that lead to the slide of the house. "I honestly didn't think we was goin' get away with that shit. My gut was feeling uneasy the whole time."

"Shit, I knew we was goin' get that off as soon as y'all put me on." Phenöm replied, just a step ahead of her with a blue and black bookbag on his back. Still in his right hand was his Desert Eagle.

"And how the fuck you know that, genius?" Chämp questioned, his heart still racing with nervousness, as he followed behind Doug who was also carrying a bookbag on her back.

"Fuck you mean? The moment that y'all told me, I knew a real nigga was goin' be in the vicinity! That's how, motherfucka." Phenöm shot back, as the 3 of them reached the driveway of the house and spotted Troy parked at the end of the driveway in a rented Buick Regal LS.

"This nigga!" Chämp said under his breath, as they walked out into the front yard.

"Y'all niggas hurry up 'fore we ---" Troy began, before they all heard shots ringing out from across the street.

"Shit!" Chämp gasped, as his body went into a complete circle before he hit the ground. A bullet ripped into Chämps left arm, causing him to say, "Fuck!"

"Get in the fucking car now!" Phenöm barked at Doug, firing his .45 back while going to check on Chämp. "You good?"

"I'm hit, nigga!"

"Come on, y'all!" Troy yelled, as bullets tore into the Regal causing Doug and Troy to duck down.

"Open the door!" Phenöm shot back, shooting Kart while trying to help Chämp to his feet.

"Nah, nigga, y'all ain't going nowhere!" Unfi yelled, as Phenöm shot Tuppa who was standing behind Unfi.

"Hurry up!" Doug shrieked, as Chämp jumped into the passenger seat.

Phenöm stood beside the Regal aiming over the roof of the car, letting off three more shots, before telling Troy, "Go head, let's get outta here!"

Tuesday December 28th, 2017

Slick's Tavern

12:11 a.m.
Nye Avenue
■ Newark ■

'If I see you and I don't speak/ that means I don't fuck with you/ I'm a boss, you a worker, bitch/ I make bloody moves/ now she says she gon' do what to who?/ let's find out and see, Cardi B/ you know where I'm at/ you know where I be/ you in the club just to party/ I'm there, I get paid a fee/ I be in and out them banks so much/ I know they're tired of me/ Honestly, don't give a fuck..........'

"Gotdamn, Girl!" DJ Cafe screamed into the microphone, mixing in Cardi B's *Bodak Yellow* so that his voice could be heard. "I need me a motherfucking kitty like that one!"

'They see pictures, they say, "goals"/ bitch, I'm who they tryna be/ look, I might just chill in some Bape/ I might just chill with your boo/ I might just feel on your babe/ my pussy feel like a lake/ he wanna swim with his face/ I'm like, "Okay"/ I'll let him do what he want/ he buy me Yves Saint Laurent/ and the new whip/ when I go fast as a horse/ I got the trunk in the front/ I'm the hottest in the street/ know you prolly heard of me..........'

"Ayo, we seriously need to have a talk, son." Phenöm said, leaning in closer so that Jünior could hear him over the music.

"What the fuck you talking about now?" he returned, tossing a few singles to Kitty as she came down the pole, ass cheeks jiggling freely.

"What the fuck you goin' do 'bout money?"

"You pick right now for us to have this conversation?" Jünior asked, hating that he had to take his eyes off of the gorgeous Kitty as he turned to face his friend.

"Fuck you talking 'bout, nigga? Anytime is the right time to talk 'bout money!" Phenöm shot back, trying not to get mad with Jünior. "I know yo ass tired of fucking living off of me, Nya, and Paul."

"Living off y'all?!" Jünior gasped, raising his voice just a little too much because he was appalled.

"Bruh, you know I ain't gonna sugar coat shit to mend your feelings. You living off us, dawg, and I know you can see it. Before ya pops got bagged, you was off your shit, now you just off!"

Even though Kitty was up on stage shaking her ass and titties, Mustafa *Jünior* Raheem II had to stop and take a look at what his brother from a different mother was saying. Christopher *Ghoon* Tate sat there face deep in a dancer's ass, wondering why they were wasting time talking with all of this ass walking around. As mad as he wanted to get, he couldn't. Whenever Jünior needed bread *[money]* he would call Nya or Phenöm, and they would come running. When Johnathan *Phenöm* Coleman was locked up, Jünior went to Nya and Paul for money, sometimes even leaning on Doug.

Fahim getting locked up changed a lot of things for Jünior, he no longer had the passion to sell drugs. And then he had Ciara now, so he wanted to be there for her instead of being locked behind bars. Nonetheless, Phenöm was right and

Jünior knew that he was leeching just a bit too much. That's the reason he had a trick up his sleeve that would set them straight for a minute, and they didn't have to sell drugs. Jünior was a faithful and firm believer of Islam, so no matter what he was doing, he would stop to offer salat [prayer]. He had been Muslim since the very day that he was born, however, he didn't really take to his deen until he was maybe around 6-years old. Within those trying years he had a bag full of blessings that changed his outlook on life, he would never again challenge nor question the mercy of, Allah *[God]*.

"Look, me and Doug got some shit lined up where we all goin' be good. This spot is a gold mine and we about to go digging!" Jünior replied, now cutting his eyes back at Kitty before her set was over. "I need to be home for this shit, that's why I'm chilling regular, I don't wanna sell drugs no more."

"Yeah aight, nigga, I'm just letting you know that you draining my pockets. Cynt down my back all the time 'bout talking to you but I didn't wanna say shit."

"But you just did!" Jünior shot back, taking a sip of his drink.

"Cause, nigga! I went in my motherfucking stash and saw my shit was 2 times shorter than it should be."

"Aight, nigga, I got it, I'ma chill regular on asking for shit." Jünior laughed, glad that Phenöm had gotten that off his chest because now he could get back to the reason they were there, the ladies!

"Yeah aight, yo ass just want me to shut up." Phenöm returned, nudging Jünior as Shopper waltzed over in search of tips and more.

"Shit I know I do!" Ghoon yelled, sitting to Jünior's right with his back turned, getting a lap dance.

"This nigga." Phenöm laughed, as Shopper walked up and slid between his legs.

"That you, babygirl!" Ghoon yelled, tossing a few singles Shopper's way.

"Y'all niggas shot the fuck out." Jünior laughed, grabbing his drink and taking a sip.

Across the bar watching the trio like a hawk, was BigDeal and LilGuy. They'd been coming to Slick's scoping out big players to rob, and tonight Jünior and his crew fit the bill. There were other dudes in the bar that have some dollars tucked away, however, they weren't easy targets. Jünior and his crew looked like they were easy peasy, so the heat was on. BigDeal was going to sit right there all night until Jünior and his crew left, and then he was going to make his move.

Shopper took Phenöm by the hand and escorted him to the bathroom, Ghoon got up and followed right behind them. Once they were inside of the bathroom, Ghoon took a seat right there at the bar in front of the bathroom. Jünior shook his head and continued drinking, until Kitty walked up and slid between his legs. She'd been watching him all night and she noticed how he was really sitting there thinking about her, so she brought it all to him. Jünior quickly straightened his back on the stool, and let Kitty's smooth skin caress his as she began to grind up against him.

To Jünior's left were the Brim homies, they were about 6 deep sitting in the front at the bar near the entrance. Hak Brim and HardBody Brim were in the middle of the wolf pack, throwing singles and popping bottles. They really had the club moving over on that end, living it up, taking pictures and/or going live on Instagram. Dante and Nazi were over by the pool table with their crew from Plainfield, throwing money away with ease. To their left were a few 793 homies and then Sul, Boyn, Larry, and Laavell. There were other dudes scattered around the bar, but these were the ones standing out.

"Damn, this shit packed." Marley said, stepping into Slicks with Brite Shine and Drop Shine in tow.

"Word, this shit," Drop Shine began before spotting the Hak Brim to their left. "Ayo, what the them faggot ass niggas doing here!?"

"Man, fuck that shit." Marley replied, tapping Drop Shine as one of the brim homies spotted them. "Let's just go have a drink."

"Fuck you mean, nigga?!" Brite Shine joined in, as the brim homie tapped the brim homie next to him alertingly.

"Yo, we just got here my nigga, them niggas ain't worried about us."

"Nah, we goin' be outside, bruh, get yo lil drink and come the fuck on. We goin' hit the Doll House up."

"Aight." Marley replied, his face telling the whole story.

Marley was out in Newark hanging with his cousin Drop Shine. So of course he wanted to hit the city while he was out there. However, Marley wasn't aware of how shit went down in Newark, he handled beef differently. And then on top of that fact, Marley wasn't in a gang, so he didn't know about 1 for all and all for 1. But he would learn today!

"*Damn, ole girl thick as shit!*" Marley thought to himself, as NannaSplit walked past him in her pink rope outfit. Just as he reached the seat that Ghoon was sitting in, his phone started ringing. He looked down at it, saw the name Tosha, and sent her to voicemail, before blurring out loud, “Go the fuck to bed already!”

“Huh?” Jünior returned, turning in his direction.

“Nah, nothing, I wasn’t talking to you.”

“Oh aight.” Jünior replied, turning around to Kitty still slow grinding on his erection to Trey Songz’s *Can’t Be Friends*.

Marley gave Jünior a dirty look, turned towards the bar, started bopping to the beat, and yelled, “Bartender!”

‘Hey, ain’t no telling what we could’ve been [ain’t no tellin what we could’ve been, no]/ and if I knew it ends like this/ I never would’ve kissed you cause I fell in love with you/ we never would’ve kicked it/ girl, every thing’s different/ I’ve lost my own recoverin’ my friend/ I wish we never did it..........’

In the bathroom, Shopper was down on her knees, sucking the skin off Phenöm’s dick. She had cardboard laid down on the floor so that she wasn’t knee deep in bathroom floor piss. Phenöm didn’t give a fuck how many times Shopper had pulled this off tonight in the same spot, you coldn’t beat $20.00 for some head [oral sex]. And then Shopper’s head at that! Yeah, Phenöm went in for the kill, dishing out a quick $60.00, and Shopper sucked the $60.00 right out of his young ass!

To her surprise, Phenöm picked her up, took a condom out and slid into it, and then dipped into Shopper’s pussy. It wasn’t a part of the package deal but once he was in there, there was no way she was going to kick him out! Shopper grabbed hold of Phenöm’s back and pulled him closer for better friction. She had to admit, the little nigga had a nice little stroke. Phenöm wasn’t even thinking about Shopper as he was deep inside of her, his mind was on Kitty! He was in there dogging Shopper's pussy, thinking about another stripper.

BANG, BANG, BANG, BANG!!!!!

"Yo, hurry up!" Boyn yelled, after banging on the door from the outside, interrupting Shopper and Phenöm.

"Nigga, go piss outside!" Phenöm replied, still stroking in and out of Shopper's wet pussy.

"Motherfucke ---"

BLOCKA, BLOCKA, BLOCKA -----
BOK, BOK, BOK, BOK, BOK -----

"Shit!" Boyn gasped, dropping to the floor while pulling his gun out from his waistline.

"What the fuck!" Phenöm gasped, diving to the floor reaching for his gun, he didn't have it.

"Oh my God!" Shopper expressed, rolling off of the sink and onto the toilet.

All that they could hear was a lot of thumping along with people screaming frantically. Phenöm checked his torso to make sure that he wasn't hit by a bullet, and then he thought about Ghoon and Jünior. Quickly and swiftly hopping into his pants as he jumped up from the floor, Phenöm was charged. He rushed out of the bathroom in time to see Hak Brim running out of the bar with his gun still aimed high.

"Yo, come the fuck on!" Ghoon yelled, still crotched down behind the bar now facing Phenöm.

"Everybody calm down and stay where you're at." DJ Cafe said over the mic, looking for the bodyguards. "Berto, get the girls and take them to the back."

"Say no more, I'm on it." Berto returned, turning towards Moore, and said, "Come on, let's get these bitches to safety."

Phenöm grabbed Ghoon and made his way out of Slicks, looking for Jünior the entire way. Everybody was forceful but hesitant to leave the bar, Phenöm and Ghoon pushed their way right through. When they got outside, Jünior was already in Nya's green 1999 Honda Accord LS waiting out front. BigDeal was in the cut trying to get to his car so that he could follow them. However the crowd was getting thicker as more people filed out of the bar. Jünior made a right up Nye Avenue ad got them the fuck out of there! Inside of the Accord the trio was now laughing about what had just taken place, as Ghoon and Jünior filled Phenöm in on what happened.

"The nigga came back inside to get his mans, started arguing with the bouncer, whipped out, and the shit went left." Ghoon informed, recalling what he saw, as Jünior made a right onto Grove Street.

"Nah, I was sitting right next to the nigga that dude was with. Son was calling the nigga sitting next to me, telling him to come on, and shit." Jünior said, remembering everything that he heard. "One of Hak's boys said something to him and he left back out." he continued, driving through the light of the Clinton Avenue intersection. "A few seconds later I hear the nigga telling the bouncer that he just need to grab his cousin from the bar. As soon as the bouncer let that nigga in, he whipped out and that's when Hak's man's whipped out. And there you have the shootout."

"Damn, I ain't even know them niggas was still beefing." Phenöm laughed, as Jünior made a right down Springfield Avenue headed to the weed spot on Ellis Avenue.

"Yo, stop at McDonalds." Ghoon told Jünior, as they were nearing the fast food restaurant.

"Nah, fuck that, we going to White Castles." Phenöm returned, looking over at Jünior. "Just go to the weed spot so we can get back to the hood, shit looking crazy tonight."

"I'm feeling that." Jünior replied, thinking about how close he was to dying tonight because the shooters were just shooting blindly.

"Of course you do, oh scary ass nigga!" Ghoon clowned from the backseat, hating how they got when they were together.

"At least you know." Jünior said, driving past McDonalds.

Slick's Tavern

3:12 a.m.
Nye Avenue
▪ Newark ▪

"This has to be the dumbest shit I've ever seen." Ofc. Perkins hissed, standing in front of Slicks.

"Aye, they say pussy brings out the best in people." Ofc. Harvey joked, preparing to walk over and question the victim.

"Ha, ha, ha, real funny."

"I'm saying, if you take everything to the heart, you'll be laid out dead just like them."

"Whatever, just go question the victim, while I go question the owner and staff."

"Roger that captain!" Ofc. Harvey shot back, saluting Ofc. Perkins before spinning on his heels heading in the victim's direction.

Thankfully only 1 person was shot tonight, there's usually multiple injuries with fatal endings. Not tonight! There was only 1 and he was alive and stable, what a break. Ofc. Harvey walked up to the ambulance with his notepad already out. However, he could see on the young man's face that he wasn't going to get much from him. At the sight of Ofc. Harvey the victim immediately scrunched his face up and turned his head. Nobody and mean nobody wanted to ever be seen talking to police, victim or not!

"How's he doing?" Ofc. Harvey asked, looking at the victim but talking to the paramedic.

"He's gonna live, the bullet went straight through. A few stitches and he'll be ready to go." Michelle replied, wrapping the victim's arm. "Do you need him?"

"Actually, I do, I have a few question I would like to ask him." Ofc. Harvey returned, walking closer to the victim. "What's your name, son?"

"Oh, you my daddy now?" the kid snapped, as he poked his chest out at Ofc. Harvey. "Man, I don't know shit! I was home having a drink and the next thing I know I got shot."

"So, you live at a gentleman's bar?

"That's the crazy thing about it, I don't know how I got here. Guess I had 1 too many drinks, huh?"

"That's your story and you're sticking with it?"

"Yup! Now, poof, be gone, offenser!" he said, waving Ofc. Harvey off with his good arm pronouncing Ofc. wrong on purpose.

"Okay, now we're gonna start over the right way, the way I prefer since you wanna be a fuckboy!" Ofc. Harvey snapped, putting his notepad away and resting his hand on his gun. "Let me see some identification, smart ass! Now!"

"Come on, bruh, you on some bullshit, I got shot and now you want my ID?"

"I'm still waiting."

While Ofc. Harvey was grilling the victim, Sergeant Nunez pulled up in her black 2016 Dodge Durango along with her partner Ford, who happened to be driving. Sergeant Nunez was actually out with Lola and Kathi having dinner and drinks at Lookers Gentlemen's Club on Dowe Avenue in Elizabeth, New Jersey. Ford on the other hand was at Breathless out in Rahway, New Jersey On Hart Street.

Ford was getting his dick sucked by one of the dancers. Breathless was a married man's dream because you had a bar where you could not only see ass but get some as well! Sergeant Nunez walked over to where Ofc. Perkins was questioning the owner, she dealt with him more so because she was more familiar with Ofc. Perkins.

"I'm telling you Ofc., I have never seen these guy up in here before in my life." States lied, standing there with her bouncers backing her up with their presence just feet away.

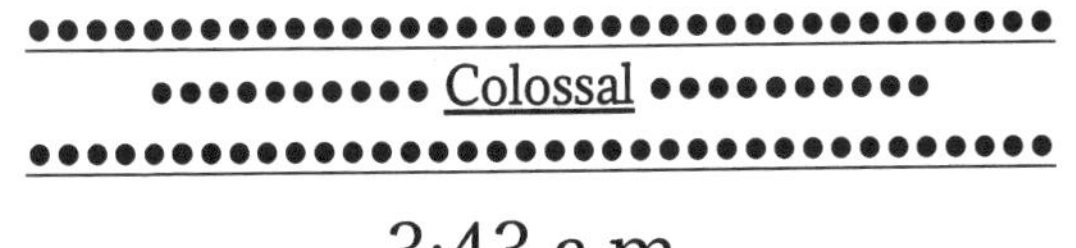

3:43 a.m.

Farley Avenue
■ Newark ■

"Yo, ya cousin mad soft, son." Phenöm clowned, as they walked into Jünior's apartment.

The apartment was a simple 2th floor apartment, with more than enough space and room for Jackie, Jünior, and her youngest son Amir *Mir* Wilder. Upon walking into the apartment, Jackie's room was straight ahead, to your immediate right was the closet of a room that Ghoon slept in. to the right of that door was the living room entryway, there was no door for the living room. Around the corner was Jackie's room, and then a long hallway that led to the kitchen and the back porch.

Across from Jackie's room to the right a little bit was Mir's room, and down the hall closer to the kitchen on the same side was Jünior's room. Across from Jünior's room to the left a little bit was the bathroom, just before the kitchen. Lianne *Lee* Tate and her kids were staying with Jaqueline *Jackie* Wilder, because they had nowhere else to go. So, Lee took the back porch which was a decent size, just enough room for her. Phenöm really didn't stay there much, he was either at Cynt's house or another one of his girlfriend's houses.

"Man, leave Chämp alone, he be in his own world sometimes." Jünior shot back, taking up for his cousin."He's harmless."

"I know! That's what I'm saying! The nigga funny style, I'm telling you right now I wouldn't put my life in that nigga's hands."

"You doing the most right now." Jünior laughed, as they walked down the hallway towards the kitchen.

Shamod *Chämp* Bowman had met them at McDonalds by accident, it just so happens that they all thought alike from time to time. So they met bumped heads at McDonalds and Chämp got into it with some dude. Instead of them fucking the dude up, Chämp walks out without getting his food. Phenöm was pissed beyond being pissed, he wanted to do something to the guy, but Chämp wasn't even fighting his own battle. Phenöm felt like Chämp was only rolling with them because he was related to Jünior.

"I'm not sucking nobody's dick for a cheeseburger!" Jackie blurted out, talking on the phone with Brenda as Lee sat next to her just as Phenöm and Jünior stepped into the kitchen.

"Nah, she's doing the most!" Phenöm shot back, bursting into laughter.

"So, this is really what y'all talk about when we're not around?" Jünior questioned, as Phenöm broke out into stomach bending laughter.

"Ain't nobody tell your ass to be eavesdropping!" Brenda shot back through the phone, causing Lee to burst into laughter.

"That's what you get for being in grown folk's business!" Lee continued to laugh, before sipping her hot chocolate.

"Huh?" Jünior gasped, looking from the phone to his aunt Lee.

"That's what yo ass get!" Phenöm clowned, leaning on the wall because his legs were weak.

"I know that's right." Brenda returned, backing her friends.

"Bren, let me call you back." Jackie said, picking her phone up from the table.

"Nah, I'm taking my old ass to bed, I'ma talk to y'all tomorrow." Brenda replied, before hanging up without waiting for a response.

"Maannnn, what y'all old women doing up this late?" Jünior asked, kicking his sneakers off and flinging them near his bedroom door.

"Fuck we goin' to bed for, ain't like we got no motherfucking jobs!" Lee shot back, causing Phenöm and Jackie to laugh even harder.

"You know what?" Jünior replied, shaking his head, understanding where Phenöm gets it from.

"What, lil nigga?" she shot back again, always quick on her toes.

"Nothing, yo, I'ma just go get in the shower cause I see y'all lit tonight." he returned, bowing down as he spun on his heels and retreated to the bathroom.

"Your father called twice for you." Jackie yelled, picking her cigarette up out of the ashtray and lighting it.

"And!?" Jünior shot back, not the least bit interested in anything that his father had to say.

"I don't know why you ducking his calls like he won't send somebody to this motherfucka looking for you." she said, taking a pull of the Newport. "You might as well gone and talk to him and get the shit outta the way. I swear y'all 2 motherfuckas is just alike, always tryna block a motherfucka out y'all lives!"

Jünior stood in the bathroom doorway with 1 foot in and 1 foot out, and said, "You only want me to talk to that nigga so he can send you ya lil finder's fee!"

"Boyyy, don't make me beat shit down ya leg!" Lee jumped in, getting to him before Jackie could say another word.

"Awww shit!" Phenöm joined in, standing against the refrigerator witnessing Jünior dig his self deeper and deeper.

"I'm saying, this ain't Where's Waldo." he said, causing Lee to launch the paper shaker at him. "That's why you missed." Jünior sang, sticking his head back out the door frame after digging in the bathroom when Lee threw the pepper shaker.

"You better go wash yo funky ass 'fore you get fucked up!" Jackie yelled, laughing as she talked.

"Don't hate me cause I'm beautiful." he said, slipping back into the bathroom.

"Can't stand his motherfuckin ass!" Lee laughed, as she sat back down turning her attention to her son. "And where the fuck y'all coming from?"

Tuesday January 4th, 2018

12:45 p.m.

Farley Avenue

■ Newark ■

"Allahu akbar *[Allah, is the greatest],*" Jünior said, before he raised his hands up to his ears, then bent over leveling his head with his back coming into ruku. Jünior placed his hands on his knees making sure to spread his fingers, his eyes focused on his prostration. "Subhana Rabbiyal 'Aadheem [*Glory is to my lord, the almighty*]."

Jünior was a faithful and firm believer of Islam, so no matter what he was doing, he would stop to offer salat [prayer]. He had been Muslim since the very day that he was born, however, he didn't really take to his deen until he was maybe around 6-years old. Within those trying years he had a bag full of blessings that changed his outlook on life, he would never again challenge nor question the mercy of, Allah [God].

Jünior stood there in his closet dressed in a dark gray T-shirt that hung down to his shins which was his Islamic garbs, underneath were a pair of black Sean John linen pants. Jünior used his closet for salat because there were neither windows nor pictures within, just his Qur'an and his musalla *[prayer rug].*

"Sami' Allahu Liman Hamidah *[Allah, listens to him, who praises him],*" Jünior said, raising back up to a standing position, before continuing, "Rabbana Wa Lakal Hamd *[Our lord, praise is for you only]*, Allahu akbar."

Sitting in Jünior's bedroom on his full size bed was, Shenya *Nya* Mathews, Jünior's best friend since he was 4-years old. Many people thought that Nya was Jünior's girlfriend, but she was just his Godsister. Nya stood 5'0" with the facial essence of the beautiful model Melyssa Ford. They understood the boundaries that shouldn't be crossed. Nya didn't really have a religion so to say but she believed that there was a God, however, she had the utmost respect for Islam thanks to Jünior, Phenöm, and Chämp.

"Daddy, paying?" 13-month old Ciara asked, trying to pronounce praying, showing her innocence as she sat on Nya's lap eating a pear.

"Yup, your daddy is in there praying for all of us." Nya replied, looking deep into the beautiful chocolate eyes of her niece.

"Llah bar!" Ciara cheered, trying to say Allahu Akbar.

"Good girl." Nya smiled, hugging Ciara tight against her chest, kissing her on top of her head lovingly.

Nya sat there in a silver Sean John velour suit with a pair of black on black low top Nike Air Force Ones, as Ciara sat on her lap with her red Juicy Couture sundress with her Pampers pull-up sticking out of the bottom. Nya loved Ciara as if she had spent 10 months within her womb instead of Armani's, and she respected Jünior highly for stepping up to the plate and being a father at 18-years old.

When the test came back that Jünior was actually 99.9 percent Ciara's father, Jünior gracefully took his daughter in. Jackie, who was Jünior's mother had flipped out when her son came home with an infant talking about he was the father, she was livid! After seeing Ciara and how much she actually looked like Jünior and herself, Jackie warmed up to Ciara and the thought of having her around.

One day when Jackie was out trying to cop some dope [heroin] from favorite dope spot she was arrested on drug charges and spent eight months in the county jail, which helped her kick her dope habit. While Jackie was in jail Nya and Phenöm had helped Jünior with watching Ciara and his then 5-year old brother, Mir. Nya had a job at Wendy's and Phenöm was in the streets selling crack cocaine alongside Jünior.

"Bismillaahir Rahmaanir Raheem, Qul A' Udhubi Rabbin Naas, Malikin Naas, Ilaahin Naas, Min Sharril Waswaasil Khannaas, Alladhee Yuwaswisu Fee Sudoorin Naas, Minal Jinnati Wan Naas *[In the name of, Allah, the most beneficent, the most merciful, say: I seek refuge with the lord and cherisher of mankind, the king of mankind, the God of mankind, from the evil of the sneaking whisperer, who whispers into the hearts of the mankind, from among the jinns and man].*" Jünior recited in Arabic, chanting Soorah An Naas.

As Jünior stood in his closet offering Asr, which starts the mid-afternoon and ends at sunset, Jackie was walking into the apartment with Mir in tow. Mir had just been suspended from school for attacking his gym teacher, kicking him in his groin because he was too tall to punch in his face. Jackie was livid about having to go pick him up because that meant that she had to leave her couch, it had nothing to do with him getting in trouble at school. The faculty at the school was under the assumption that Jackie was mad because her child had assaulted his teacher, but they were way off from the truth.

Jackie was pissed because she had to get up in the middle of her daytime show *The Wendy Williams Show*, cutting into her drinking time. Since Ciara had come into her life, Jackie had kicked the drugs so to say and began drinking daily. Her favorite drinks were Bud Light and E&J VSOP Brandy, and she would sit in front of the television watching show after show getting drunker by the commercial.

"Take your lil ass in your room and don't dare turn on that TV or that PlayStation!" Jackie barked, sitting down on her green suede couch, while kicking off her gray Reebok Classics. Reaching for her beer and cigarette all in one motion.

"Whatever." Mir mumbled, walking down the hallway headed towards his room.

"What!?"

"Nothing, ma."

"That's what the fuck I thought, cause I'll run smooth up in your shit," she yelled, causing Nya to step out of Jünior's room with Ciara dead on her heels. "Y'all lil fucker's think that I'm some kind of joke around this motherfucka!"

"Jackie," Nya called out, sticking her head into the living room. "Mustafa is in there offering salat!"

"Gandma, daddy in here paying." Ciara chimed in, mispronouncing words as she was holding on tightly to the doorframe.

"Hey, Ciara, come and give grandma some sugar." Jackie replied, ignoring Nya while sitting her cigarette down, holding her arms open for her grand baby.

Ciara stumbled towards Jackie with a huge smile on her face, revealing just how loved she was by the woman sitting there raising hell at Mir. One thing that couldn't be denied was the love that Jackie had for that little girl, Ciara was Jackie's everything and there was nothing she wouldn't do for her. Whenever Ciara was in the same room with Jackie, you saw a much softer and sweet side to Jackie. Though Jackie was not proud that Jünior had had a baby at such a young age, Jackie was thankful that her grand baby was there and healthy. Jackie knew that Armani was getting high when she was pregnant with Ciara, a few times Jackie had even gotten high with Armani. So Jackie was extremely thankful that Ciara came out with no complications whatsoever, she was truly a blessing.

"As salaamu alaikum wa rahmatullah *[Peace and mercy of, Allah, be on you].*" Jünior recited, with his head turned towards his right, sitting on both of his legs, his left leg under him while his right leg remained upright. Both his hands were on his knees, fingers spread open, as he turned his head to the left. "As salaamu alaikum wa rahmatullah."

Jünior pressed his balled up fist against his musalla, pushing his way up to a standing position, he turned and walked to the door, leaving his musalla where it was. When he stepped out of the closet he spotted Mir instead of Nya and Ciara, Mir looked up and greeted him, "As salaamu alaikum, Jünior."

"Wa alaikum as salaam wa rahmatullah," Jünior returned, removing his Islamic garbs before neatly folding them up. "What are you doing home so early?"

"Mr. Blue kept talking shit so I kicked his faggot ass in the dick, and I got suspended for a week."

"Damn, Amir, you only been back in school for two weeks!" he returned, as Nya walked back into the room.

"Jackie gets on my nerves, yo, word up!" Nya announced, holding her white Galaxy S2 in her left hand.

"Whose nerves doesn't she get on?" Mir replied, turning on Jünior's PlayStation.

"Where's Ciara?" Jünior questioned, looking behind Nya for her shadow.

"She's in the living room with her *gandma*, watching Ghost Whisperer."

"Aight, let's get outta here before either of them realize that we're gone." Jünior said, laughing at Nya's impersonation of the way that Ciara pronounced grandma, as he grabbed his burgundy New Era 59 Fifty Newark Brick City fitted off of his dresser.

Mir shook his head as Jünior and Nya quickly snuck out of the house without Jackie hearing them, this was something he did every time that Ciara had his mother's attention. The 2 of them walked out of the front door of the 3-family house in which Jünior stayed in, which was located on Madison Avenue in between 18th Street and 17th Street. It was closer towards 18th Street about four houses down from the corner, a place they had been residing for the past four years. Jünior led Nya across 18th Street towards Clinton Avenue where they were going to wait for the number 13 bus, coming from Irvington Terminal.

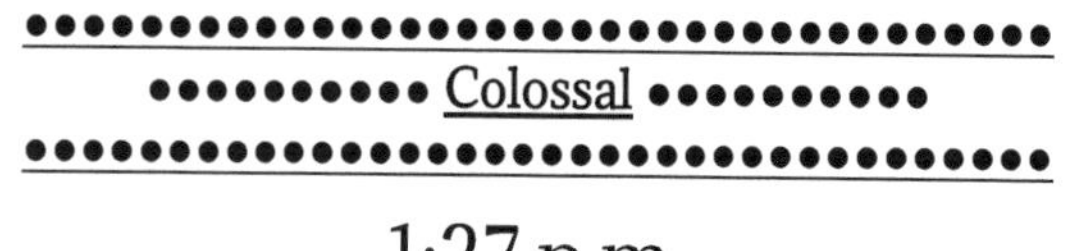

1:27 p.m.

Chadwick Avenue
▪ Newark ▪

"What's in the bank?" Phenöm asked, as he held nine $20 bills in his left hand, standing amongst his peers on the corner of Madison Avenue, behind building 100.

"It's umm ---" Doug started, looking down at the ground quickly counting the money that lie there in front of them. "It's $74.00 in there."

"Stop it!" Phenöm shot back, cockily as he stood there shifting through a stack of bills..

Doug looked up at Phenöm and shook her head, "Aight, let's get it then."

Chadwick Avenue was crowded with people from one end to the next, from Clinton Avenue all the way back down to Avon Avenue. Women, children, drug addicts, teens, drug dealers, and gang bangers populated the streets of Chadwick Avenue. Renee *Doug* Corey and the family as they called themselves were posted up on the corner that most of them grew up on for majority of their lives. Doug picked the dice back up and started shaking them in her right balled up fist, as everybody looked on with anticipation. Phenöm knew that Doug couldn't really roll dice so he was trying to come up off of her, after he had already won $40.00 from her and $25.00 from Troy.

Doug stood there with a smile on her face, wearing a pair of light blue Seven jeans, a red short sleeve Galaxy T-shirt, and a pair of black on black Nike Air Max. Atop Doug's head was a red and black New Era 59 fifty New Jersey fitted, tilted to the side with much swag. Doug looked like a heavier tomboy version of the singer, Ciara. Even with the extra weight Doug was still a cute girl in a rough shell. Doug was the oldest member of the family being 21-years old, and out of all nine of the members Doug had the purest heart.

"I got $20.00 that say Doug ace up again." Sofi said, looking at each face standing to her left and right.

"Bitch, you must be in the mood to be giving out free money!" Doug spat, tossing a $20.00 bill on the ground in front of Sofi's feet, still shaking the three dice in her left hand.

"Shit, let a bitch get in on that bet!" Paul joined in, tossing two $10.00 bills on the ground as well.

"Hey, it ain't no fun if the homies can't have none!" Tàbi laughed, pulling a stack of $1.00 and $5.00 bills out of her bra, itching for some of the betting action.

"Man, fuck that, Doug, roll the motherfucking dice!" Phenöm said, losing the little bit of patience that he had.

The family consisted of 9 wild ass girls that thrived off of doing everything that a dude could do, looking out for one another. There was Doug, Tàbi, Nique, Rae, Troy, Nya, Mona, Lissa, and Chelia. They were the young crew out there on Chadwick Avenue which the bloods gave respect to because they went hard for theirs, and on top of that they were buying work off of the big homie of the bloods sect, 7re.

Doug quickly released the dice against the step outside of the back door of building 100, which was on the corner of Chadwick Avenue and Madison Avenue. The dice beat against the wall as a black Dodge Magnum pulled right up on the corner undetected, the occupants of the Magnum were watching the dice game from behind the tinted windows.

The blood homies that were in the middle of the block slowly noticed the Magnum.

However, they thought nothing of it because dudes were always pulling up to the corner to holler at one of the girls. Fiends walked pass with their minds stuck on getting high or coming up with a scheme to get high, hustling hard for that fix! Children ran rapidly throughout the block enjoying the years awarded to them to be a kid, jumping rope and/or riding their bikes in the street.

"Tracy!" Doug yelled, throwing her arms in the air after the dice landed on two 1's and 3.

"I can beat a 3 with my eyes closed and both of my hands tied behind my back." Phenöm exclaimed, bending down to pick up the dice, as Doug picked up her side bet money.

As the dice game was going on, Jünior and Nya were walking from Clinton Avenue, laughing at the guy on the bus. This guy was high off of crack cocaine and he was on the bus singing Jazmine Sullivan for everybody. Jünior made jokes saying that he was singing to Nya, which pissed her off for a moment. By the time that they got off of the bus, Nya wasn't mad anymore. As they walked towards building 100, they spoke to everybody that they passed by.

"As salaamu alaikum, Ahki *[my brother].*" Mr. Studie greeted, sitting in front of building 100 as Chämp stepped through the doors.

"Wa alaikum as salaam," Chämp returned, looking across the street to his right at Lincoln Fried Chicken which was closed. Turning his head back towards the front of him, he noticed a red Family cab pull up to the curb. "What's it looking like out here, Mr. Studie?"

"What can I say, it's the same damn Bergen Street!"

"Yeah, it's the same thing every day and every day we look for something new with no results."

"Rob, come help me with Monique so that I can take these bags outta the trunk, this stupid motherfucka wild'n!" Nique explained, standing outside of the cab holding the back door open, where Chämp could see little Monique sitting in her pink and black Gerber car seat.

"Damn shame, them foreigners be acting like they better than everybody!" the older lady, Mrs. Baker, expressed, sitting on a dingy orange beach chair outside of the fence surrounding the building.

"Shit, tell me about it!" Ms. Willis joined in, looking down through her eyeglasses.

"Aight, here I come." Chämp replied, knowing how the older women that sat in front of the building could get.

16-year old Chämp was what you called a venomous brain, he was mentally dangerous for his age, and could be fairly as dangerous with his hands. Chämp stood 5'4", weighing 130lbs., a honey roasted brown skin complexion, with an I.Q. of 125 which was pretty high with the highest being 170. It was Jünior who started calling him Chämp because of all of the Scrabble that Chämp had managed to win over the years since he was about 8-years old, it was pretty scary how Chämp was able to out spell men four times his age. Chämp wasn't street savvy the way that Jünior was because he wasn't into the things that Jünior had been exposed to at such a young age, however, Chämp wasn't your every day push over.

Chämp and Jünior were cousins through marriage on his mother's side, and one could say that they were as close as brothers on most days. Chämp was originally from Millville,

New Jersey, but at the age of 7 Chämp was shipped up to Newark to live with his uncle because of the living arrangement with his mother. She couldn't afford to keep her child, which meant that Chämp had to be shipped up north to stay with her brother whom didn't have any kids at the time. Chämp's uncle was married to Asia's sister, Trinice, and Asia was Jünior's uncle Akbar's wife.

Chämp walked over towards the cab as Jünior and Nya were coming down the street from Clinton Avenue, so heavy in their conversation that they'd been having since they left the house. Chämp leaned into the cab and unbuckled Monique's seatbelt and wiggled her car seat towards him, making sure that he didn't lose his grip or footing. Nique had just come from downtown Newark buying her and Monique a bunch of clothes with her welfare check, something that she did every month on the first but her check had come late this month.

Nique was Sofi's little sister, so no doubt that Nique received the utmost respect in their hood, Sofi was the first lady of her blood sect and Sofi was surely a threat within a threat! Just as Chämp was sitting the car seat onto the sidewalk, Jünior and Nya were stepping behind Monique's car seat, Nya walked over to Nique and started helping her with her bags. Jünior and Chämp slapped one another five and embraced into a brotherly hug, something that they'd been doing for years now.

"As salaamu alaikum, cuzzo." Chämp greeted, as they broke their embrace and looked towards Monique.

"Wa alaikum as salaam wa rahmatullah wa barrakatu." Jünior responded, checking out the blue and white Jordan 12's that Chämp was wearing.

"Yeah, nigga, these joints is like that!" Chämp said, reading Jünior's thoughts, seeing where his eyes went to.

"When the fuck did you get those?"

While Chämp and Jünior were chatting it up, they began walking around the corner to the back of the building. Chämp started telling Jünior about the movement that he was trying to get going down in Millville. Though Jünior wasn't in the game, he knew a lot of good people and Chämp wanted him to reach out to one of them. However, Jünior hadn't done that for Phenöm so he damn sure wasn't about to do it for Chämp's simple ass! Jünior saw the dice game and wanted to get in, however, Nya had his money. So, him and Chämp turned around to go get his money from Nya.

"This nigga aced up!" Troy laughed, after Phenöm rolled a 1 and two 6's, failing to beat Doug's 3 as Chämp and Jünior bent the corner..

"Shit, I should've been betting against this nigga" Sofi announced, as the front and back passenger doors of the Magnum flew open, releasing BigDeal and Lil Guy.

"I wish you would've, and then maybe I would've beaten the tracy!" Phenöm replied, kicking the dice against the wall before turning around to the unraveling drama that was born to unfold. "Shit!"

"Nigga, you know what it is!" BigDeal growled, pressing the cold steel of his .9mm against the back of Tàbi's head, causing her eyes to pop out of her head.

"Aight, now let's all play nice and this will ---" Lil Guy tried to explain.

BOC, BOC, BOC !!!
POP, POP.....POP !!!

"Aaggghhhh!" Lil Guy screamed out painfully, as his body made its way to the ground, the money that he had in his hands flying into the air helplessly.

Phenöm couldn't believe that he'd been caught slipping once he spotted Lil Guy and BigDeal, his heart began to pound rapidly in his chest knowing that it only took one second for his life to quickly come to an end. Seeing Tàbi with the barrel against her head forced Phenöm to react the only way that he knew how.

His palms had gotten sweaty and his survival instincts quickly kicked into overdrive. Dowe, who was the driver of the Magnum had caught Phenöm pulling his .38 a little too late, but he was able to still grab his .380 and aim it in Phenöm's direction before letting three shots off.

In the blind of trying to duck those shots Phenöm pumped 2 of his own bullets into Lil Guy, the third bullet hitting the back door of the Magnum. Everything was happening so fast that BigDeal was stuck there with confusion, as well as the Brim and Piru homies down the street. It never registered to BigDeal to make a run for it because he just knew that this would be a sweet lick. BigDeal had yet to pull the trigger to his .9mm because he was still trying to fathom the fact that his man was on the ground motionless.

In the midst of everything Phenöm was unaware that Sofi was on the ground clutching at her chest from a gunshot wound, she was in so much pain that she couldn't even alert anyone that she was hit. Just as BigDeal was about to check on his mans a bullet flew past his ear waking him up to the situation that lie ahead.

Knowing that it was only a matter of time before the Piru homies ran up. With cat-like reflexes BigDeal quickly dove for the Magnum just barely leaving the ground landing in the back seat, the Magnum was able to pull away from the curb as BigDeal and Dowe escaped with their lives through the skin of their teeth.

Nya, Jünior, Chämp, and Nique came running around the corner towards the bullshit blindly, Nique had given Monique to Mrs. Baker to take into the building before she got hurt. The Magnum made a wild left turn up Madison Avenue as the 4 of them reached their friends.

With the most confused expressions on their faces visually trying to see if everybody was okay. Still nobody knew that Sofi was shot and the pain was so severe that she still couldn't find the voice to let them know, all she could do was lie there trying to breathe as best as she could.

"What the fuck!" Jünior yelled, as Phenöm stood directly on the corner holding his smoking .38 at his side.

"Is everybody okay?" Nya asked, as the girls started to climb back to their feet, noticing the Piru homies coming down the block with their guns drawn.

"Them motherfuckas had that fucking gun to my head!" Tàbi screamed heatedly, with tears doing a marathon down her cheeks, as she stood up and faced Nya. Onlookers stood off to the side shaking their heads, not at all impressed with the things that took place just seconds ago.

"Oh my, God, Sofia!!!" Paul yelled, being the first to realize that Sofi hadn't returned to her feet.

"Somebody call, 911!" Doug screamed dropping to her knees, finally noticing the small pool of crimson red staining the front of Sofi's pink and white short sleeve LRG T-shirt.

Jünior and Chämp were standing on the corner next to Phenöm and the trio were all giving one another the look of obviousness, they knew that they were up to bat meaning it was up to them to rectify this situation. Chämp wasn't the gangster type so he knew that he was going to have to do his part from his best point of view, he had to keep his eyes on the business at hand, and back up Jünior and Phenöm with whatever they needed.

Phenöm was just the opposite, he was definitely the nigga to get the job done at all cost, he wasn't book smart nor business savvy but he could murder without a second thought. Jünior was however swift in all of those areas, he was what most would consider a gangster and a gentleman, he was just the right dude to be in charge of something. The 3 of them stood there really not too sure of anything else other than the fact that it was on, Sofi being shot wasn't something that could *EVER* go unanswered!

Tuesday January 6th, 2018

9:31 p.m.
Dayton Street
■ Newark ■

"What the fuck are you waiting for, Mustafa!? 7re already told you what you needed to know about these motherfuckas!" Nique barked, eyes swollen from all of the crying that she had been doing today, standing in Evergreen Cemetery in her black spandex maxi dress.

"Nique, relax, we need a lil more on the situation than just who did it." Jünior replied, clutching his black iPhone 2S tightly just thinking about Sofi laid up in the hospital enduring surgeries.

"Are you fucking kidding me right now!" she yelled, as Doug put her left arm around Nique's shoulder. Nique shoved Doug's arm away and took a step back before continuing. "My fucking sister is laid up in U.M.D. fighting for her gotdamn life and you're standing around talking about you need *more* than the names of who did it! Mustafa, you on some fuckboy shit, nigga!"

"I'm on it, Dominique, I said relax." Jünior calmly told her, trying to keep from snapping out on his girl.

"Fuck you and your motherfucking relaxing, nigga! You, Shamod, and Johnnie need to handle this shit before I do!" Nique spat, then walked away leaving Chämp and Doug staring at Jünior.

"She's right, Jünior, with Lil Guy's picture and name being plastered all over the news, we didn't even need 7re to confirm who Dowe and BigDeal was." Doug said, standing against somebody's head stone holding a bottle of peach Ciroc in her right hand.

"First of all, Johnnie is outta of commission right now thanks to his carelessness. The whole Newark is looking for his ass, so we can't use him right now. Secondly, the only thing that I'm sitting back and doing is trying to tame 8 emotional ass bitches that wanna tell me how to move when I'm well capable of thinking for my motherfucking self!" Jünior spat, hurt by the way that Nique had just spoken to him. "And last but not least, I can't move on a motherfucking soul until I receive an address, phone number, or a fucking block to find them on! If I leave it up to y'all I should be out on every block shooting at anybody until I'm either shot down or hauled off in fucking handcuffs!"

Doug wasn't at all shocked at the way that Jünior was flipping out because he was known to spaz out from time to time, with Sofi being shot and Nique on a rampage she knew that Jünior was under a lot of pressure. Because Jünior and Nique were now seeing each other in an open relationship, Nique knew that by throwing herself out there to handle the situation, Jünior would get a move on it. There was no way that Jünior was going to allow Nique on the front line after everything that had just happened to Sofi.

So Jünior was going to put his all into finding BigDeal and Dowe and killing them. Bottom line was Sofi was in the hospital fighting for her young life and her sister was out here lost without her better half, Nique didn't know what she would do if Sofi didn't pull through which is why she wasn't even thinking that her sister wouldn't make it. Nique wasn't trying to come at Jünior that way, but she needed him to get a move on BigDeal and Dowe.

Phenöm was out in Hillside, New Jersey at Dina's house hiding out because he was wanted for questioning in the murder of Lil Guy, as soon as his picture was shown on TV, he took off. His fingerprints were found on one of the bullets found inside of Lil Guy, so police said that they wanted to talk to him which meant that they wanted to arrest him and quickly close the case. 7re, who happened to be Sofi's big homie let it be known that he was going to paint the town red trying to find the other two gunmen.

7re was going to let Newark know that you couldn't touch any of their homies and get away with it. Jünior had called a meeting in Evergreen Cemetery which was right next to Weequahic Park, so that he could break the news to Nique and Doug but things didn't go the way that he expected them to. Through the connections that Jünior still had from his father's trusted people that were now home, he was about to have the whereabouts on Dowe and BigDeal.

"What's our next move?" Chämp asked, knowing that Jünior had a plan that would need his strategic and methodical thinking to ensure their success.

"I'm waiting for a phone call from Koji that'll point us in the right direction as far as them 2 niggas. Doug, I need you to stay focused on that other thing, you and Troy." Jünior said, standing there in a black Sean John linen suit that Nya bought him. "I need the crew ready when it's time to move."

"And, Nique?" Doug asked.

"I got Nique, just stay focused on Troy and Tàbi, this has to be as smooth as silk when it goes down."

"And what about, Johnnie?" Chämp questioned, standing there across from Jünior dressed in a royal blue and black Enyce button-up and dark blue Levi jeans. "He can't stay in hiding for too long, I hate to admit it but we need that nigga out here."

"Call up a good defense lawyer and see how much it's going to cost to escort him down to the precinct to handle the questioning without them locking him up." he answered, rubbing his temples with his index and middle fingers, realizing that his task at hand was serious. "Doug, you get with Paul and Rae, the 3 of y'all put something up for Phenöm's lawyer."

"Aight." Doug replied, pulling her phone out to make the call immediately.

"I got $200.00 for him right now." Chämp informed, digging into his pocket to slide Jünior the change that he had in his pockets. I'll bring you more after I count my shit when I get in the crib.

"Aight, I'ma see what I can come up with in the next few hours, but y'all know that I'm limited right now." Jünior replied shamefully knowing that he should have taken the money that Sul tried to give him from Fahim..

"Don't worry about it, just take care of the Sofi situation and I'll make sure that Phenöm gets a lawyer." Doug said, ending her call with Rae. Rae and Paul on that shit right now, we'll have that bread in no time.

"Aight, bet." he returned, closing his eyes to block out the reality of the world for just a few seconds.

"Yo, breath easy, skoob, you got this. Just take Nique back to the block and let's go head hunting." Chämp said, knowing exactly what Jünior was thinking when he said the next few hours. “You ain’t going out by yourself, motherfucka.”

“Oh hell naw, we ain’t doing that, bruh.” Doug jumped in, looking at Jünior as if he was plum crazy.

11:01 p.m.
22nd STREET
▪ Newark ▪

“And you’re sure that these niggas live over here?” Jünior asked, sitting in the driver’s seat of a stolen tan Mitsubishi Galant ES, with his black iPhone 2S pressed against his left ear.

“The address that my peoples gave me is 19th and 22nd so I know that it’s legit, you go there and I guarantee you that you’re bound to run into Dowe or Deal.” Koji returned, sitting in his living room watching the movie *Basic Instinct*.

“Aight, bruh, good looking.”

“You know that I got you, lil nigga, when’s the last time that you spoke to your father?” he questioned, already knowing the answer to his own question.

“It’s been a while, but he still writes me every month, I’m just not ready to forgive him for how everything went down, you feel me? He left us out here with nothing, he left me out here to fend for myself!”

“Jünior, you could never be out here by yourself as long as I got breath in my lungs, but I understand how you feel when it comes to needing your father so I'm not going to press you on that. Just know that Fahim wasn't the greatest man or father for that matter, however, he lived for you and your brother and I know that he would love to hear from you."

"Yeah, aight, look, good looking for the heads up on that other thing, bruh." Jünior said, letting it be known that he didn't want to talk about his father right then.

"You got it, lil bruh, hit me up later so we can hit the pool hall or something."

"Aight, bruh."

Jünior hung up on Koji feeling bad that he had come off like that towards him, however, he was still angry with Fahim for leaving him the way that he did because his uncle Akbar had warned Fahim to get out, but Fahim refused so Jünior felt like his father chose the streets over him. For the past five years Fahim had been writing Jünior and Mir a letter every month, from time to time Fahim would call the house and speak to Jackie and Mir but Jünior refused to acknowledge his presence. Koji was one of Fahim's soldiers that had just come home after serving four years in the Feds, he was charged with the very minimal of charges because he was only a delivery boy as was Jünior.

Jünior and Koji had clicked after they met during one of their many deliveries, the two young boys clicked fairly quickly considering the circumstances that they were under. Koji was 7 years older than Jünior but they were mentally on the same level, Koji liked Jünior because he reminded him so much of Fahim. A lot of the dudes that were now home after serving their time that were a part of Fahim's empire were always looking out for Jünior out of respect and love for Fahim, most of them were distant friends of Jünior's.

Jünior and Phenöm sat inside of the Galant which was parked on the corner of 19th Avenue facing 22nd Street, facing the corner store across the street. Phenöm was sitting there with his navy blue Yankees fitted pulled down low over his eyes, loading his .38 revolver. He was dressed in a Blac Label T-shirt, a pair of True Religion jeans, and a pair of black on black Jordan 11's, he was ready to dead the niggas responsible for shooting Sofi. Jünior had never shot a gun let alone killed somebody but that was all about to change tonight, because he was down for that 187 in the name of his sister Sofi, he was going to pop his murder cherry tonight!

Jünior sat in the driver's seat holding a black chrome .9mm Ruger, dressed in a black Chämpion sweat suit and a pair of black ACG boots, and they both were wearing black Reebok baseball gloves. Jünior sat his S2 on his lap before reaching into his pocket and pulled out Beanie Sigel The B-Coming album, he slid it into the CD player, and turned it to track number 13 which was Sofi's favorite song. Look At Me Now was a song that Sofi listened to everyday at least ten times, she was a beautiful person but a gangstress at heart fully.

"*My hair was knotty then/ nose snotty then/ sweats, no pockets then/ sweatin', no problems then/ facts? Off the potty then/ news? watchin' karate then/ playin' double dutch,/ she was hopscotchin' then/ me girl watchin' then/ crooked little eye. [eye]/ humpback, tryna hump that/ yes I [I]/ couldn't play because I'm poo/ they thought I was mockin' them* ---" Jünior rapped, closing his eyes thinking back to the first time that he had heard Sofi playing the song.

"That movie was wack as hell!" Doug said, sitting in the passenger seat of the stolen gold 2008 Audi A6 wearing a brown Dickies one-piece jumper, as Sofi made a right turn onto Bergen Street from 16th Avenue.

"Nah, that shit was poppin', you just wack as hell." Sofi replied, lighting up a blunt of purple haze.

"Fuck outta here, bitch!"

"The movie was ass but Doug, you can be country as hell from time to time, my nigga." Jünior joined in, laughing from the back seat as Sofi pulled up to the light on Springfield Avenue.

"You know what, fuck the both of y'all, how about that!" Doug shot back, as the traffic began moving through the intersection, before a white 2007 Audi S4 hit them from the back, grabbing all of their attention.

"What the fuck!" the trio barked, turning their heads around to the back looking out of the window to see who had just rammed them.

"This bitch ass nigga." Sofi laughed, relieved that it was her homie and not the police or the train trying to force her.

"Who the fuck is that?" Jünior asked, still looking out of the back window as Sofi made a left turn onto 17th Avenue and pulled over beside Cleveland Elementary School.

"It's my homie, Alvin." Sofi answered, as the S4 pulled up next to them on the driver's side.

"What's poppin', motherfucka!?" Alvin greeted, leaning over on to the passenger seat of the S4 looking into the A6.

"What's Mob'n, nigga?"

"Tag, you're it." he laughed, before stomping on the accelerator and racing down 17th Avenue.

"This nigga play too much!" Sofi laughed, as she stomped on her accelerator and took off down 17th Avenue after him.

Sofi sped off realizeing that she couldn't let the S4 get too far ahead of her, Doug and Jünior sat back in their seats preparing for the car chase not the least bit worried because

Sofi had the wheel. Alvin raced past the precinct on the corner of 17th Avenue and Irvine Turner Boulevard, making it his business to snatch E.B.'s [emergency brakes] skidding around the corner with tire screeching loudness. Sofi was hot on his bumper when he made the left turn onto Irvine Turner Boulevard, but she didn't snatch her E.B.'s and her A6 slid around the corner just nicely. The two Audi's raced towards W. Kinney Street dipping in and out of traffic, Alvin knew that Sofi was going to bring it when he bumped her, but he was confident that his S4 could out run her A6.

While the S4 was skidding around the corner onto W. Kinney Street, Sofi was putting The B-Coming into the CD player, preparing to make the right turn just as Alvin had just done. The number 99 bus was sitting there on the corner letting passengers aboard the bus as the A6 rocked onto W. Kinney, Jünior sat in the back smiling as the A6 drifted around the corner and down the hill. Alvin was rocking a right onto Prince Street by the time that Sofi had reached the middle of the block, but she was hot on his ass.

'My hair was knotty then/ nose snotty then/ sweats, no pockets then/ sweatin', no problems then/ facts? Off the potty then/ news? watchin' karate then/ muddas playin' double dutch,/ she was hopscotchin' then/ me girl watchin' then/ crooked little eye. [eye]/ humpback, tryna hump that..........'

"He busting your ass!" Jünior pointed out, as the A6 swung onto Prince Street just in time to see the S4 rock a left down Montgomery.

"Don't worry about it, I'ma catch his ass." Sofi replied, leaning forward to see the street better, nodding her head to Look At Me Now.

"Look, Look," Jünior said, as Alvin made it look like he was about to turn onto Somerset and then threw the S4 into a 180 degree spin, now headed back towards the A6. "Oh, he showing off right now on you, Sofi."

"I see him, but watch this."

"What the fuck!" Doug gasped.

Sofi snatched E.B.'s throwing the A6 to the left just catching the back bumper of the S4 as Alvin tried to race past them.

"There that nigga go right there!" Phenöm informed, snapping Jünior back to reality when he saw BigDeal come walking out of the front door of the building that was attached to the corner store.

"Huh," Jünior blurted out, locking in on BigDeal who was wearing a white Galaxy T-shirt, a pair of Red Monkey jeans, and a pair of tan Timberlands. "Oh. Aight, let's go."

"Wait, hold up!" Phenöm ordered, as Jünior was opening his door to get out and dead BigDeal. "Look."

"Oh, shit!" Jünior said, noticing the police Ofc.s that were closing in on BigDeal from all angles.

"This has gotta be one lucky ass motherfucka!"

"He could run but he can't hide, I'll get his ass in the Monster if I have to." Jünior said, letting his frustrations be known by the tone of his voice.

Tuesday January 12th, 2018

9:18 a.m.

Chancellor Avenue

■ Newark ■

"We….declare, that these united colonies are, and of right ought to be free and independent states, that they are absolved from all allegiance to the British crown ---" Ms. Fairfell read aloud, as she stood in front of her classroom with her teacher's history book open, and her eyes glued within.

Jünior was in class, however his mind was elsewhere as he sat in the front row near the classroom door. Jünior had his text book open to the page that Ms. Fairfell was reading just as the other eleven students in the room, but his mind was on the Sofi situation. The issue had been weighing down heavy on Jünior, and the fact that Nique wasn't talking to him hurt even more.

Word on the street was out that 7re and the bloods were out to avenge their homie, still, Nique wanted the blow to come from her camp, she wanted Jünior to settle the score for Sofi. With Phenöm lying as low as he was, Jünior was in a tight spot because that meant that they could only move at night, and he didn't feel comfortable moving without Phenöm because he'd never killed anybody before.

See, Jünior used to be a runner for his father from the age of 5 all the way up until he was 13-years old, Jünior would be given a package of drugs and told where to drop them off at.

The moment that the Feds kicked in their front door and folded Fahim's operation, Jünior decided that he would do his own thing, the family, Phenöm, and Chämp all looked to him for guidance and leadership.

Though Doug and Nya were the voices of the crew and the main reason that the girls were even selling drugs, they all followed behind Jünior because he'd run with a mean group of hard hitters. No one but Nya knew that Jünior had never killed a soul, he had shot plenty of people but never killed anyone. If Jünior didn't body somebody quickly in the name of Sofi, his crew would look at him differently.

"And that all political connection between them and the state of Great Britain, is and ought to be totally dissolved, and that as free and independent states, they have full power to levy war, conclude power.....excuse me," Ms. Fairfell said, pinching the bridge of her nose, before continuing. "I mean, conclude peace, contract alliances, establish commerce, and do all other acts and things which independent states may of right do ---"

KNOCK! KNOCK! KNOCK !!!

"Yes." Ms. Fairfell answered, after she was interrupted from her reading by the knock at the classroom door.

The door slowly opened and everybody's attention in the classroom turned towards the door out of curiosity as to who it was interrupting their class. To everybody's surprise, 2 African American men in suits walked into the room escorted by 2 Caucasian men in police uniforms and the principal, Mr. Hellburch. The man in the front of the convoy raised his badge, and said, "Good morning, Ms. Fairfell, my name is Ofc. Harvey and this is my partner Ofc. Perkins."

"Ummm......good morning Ofc.s, what brings you into my classroom today?" she nervously asked, sitting her teacher's book on top of her desk.

"We have an arrest warrant for Mustafa Raheem II, in connection to a murder." Ofc. Harvey answered, holding the arrest warrant up in the air.

"A warrant? A murder? For Mustafa?"

"Yes, ma'am."

"Are you certain that you have the right person, I mean, Mustafa is a good kid and one of my best students!"

"We'll take that into consideration, Ms. Fairfell, but either way Mr. Raheem has to come with us." Ofc. Perkins returned, locking eyes with Jünior.

Jünior was at a loss for words as the two uniformed Ofc.s approached him, causing his peers to whisper comments between one another as the police put the handcuffs on him. Being wanted for murder wasn't something that ever crossed his mind, even after his father went down for running a drug empire and multiple homicides. Jünior knew damn well that he hadn't committed any murders, EVER! Once he was handcuffed he lowered his head in the infamously traditional criminal fashion, taking the walk of shame out of the classroom and right out of Weequahic High School. Principal Hellburch didn't say a word, he just allowed the police to come into his school and arrest one of his best students, the other students as well as Ms. Fairfell were looking to him for answers but he lowered his head like a coward and walked out of the classroom. He didn't have any answers for them, honestly, he was just as nervous as they were in the Dt.'s presence!

●●●●●●●●●●●●●●●●●●●●●●●●●●●●●●●●●●●

•••••••••• Colossal ••••••••••
•••••••••••••••••••••••••••••••••••

10:22 a.m.
Irvine Turner Boulevard
■ Newark ■

While Jünior was on Chancellor Avenue being arrested and stuffed into the back of a Newark Police squad car, Phenöm was out doing the devil's work when he should've been in hiding. He was down on Irvine Turner Boulevard and W. Bigelow Street sitting in a stolen brown Oldsmobile Cutlass, looking around the area peeping the scene trying to stake out his getaway. Phenöm was a middle school dropout, he grew up extremely poor with no food to eat or a place to call home.

Phenöm, his brother Ghoon, and his mother Lee lived in one abandoned house after another abandoned house as squatters, and that's how Jünior and Phenöm actually met. Jünior had been kidnapped as a kid, taken for ransom and dumped into the basement of an abandoned house on Chadwick Avenue and Hawthorne Place, feeling like his young life was surely over.

While the kidnappers were waiting for Fahim to respond to their demands, Phenöm was in the basement freeing Jünior from the rope that was tied around his wrist and ankles. Phenöm was Jünior's savior that day and because of Phenöm's heroic act Fahim gave Phenöm and his family a place to call home, and along with the apartment that Fahim paid the first two years rent up front he gave Lee, $20,000.00 That day down in the basement Jünior had to trust that Phenöm wasn't there to hurt him and in the midst of that, a bond was formed between the two of them. Now, standing 5'9", weighing 209lbs, Phenöm was anything but that little homeless kid in that abandoned basement. And the bond that the 2 of them shared after that night was amazing, they always had one another's back no matter the situation.

Climbing out of the Cutlass, Phenöm put his left hand on his waist steadying his .38, while using his right hand to close the driver door. On his head was a dreadlock wig cap, he was dressed in a Ryder's moving uniform jumper, with a pair of black Spalding baseball gloves on his hands. He made sure that he was seen by all of the people going on about their day as he walked up to the gated three-family house, and he did that by tripping over the garbage can that was sitting on the curb awaiting the garbage man.

Reaching the top step of the dark gray wooden porch, he made even more noise by whistling loudly, he was setting the tone of what he wanted any potential witnesses to see and hear. Phenöm walked up to the front door and looked to his right at the door bells where the tenants' names were located, when he saw what he was looking for he turned back around and headed back to the Cutlass. On his way down the walkway his red Samsung Galaxy S2 began to ring, he knew that it was somebody of importance because of the ring tone that was sounding off.

'Oh you got his heart and my heart and none of the pain/ you took your suitcase, I took the blame/ now I'm tryna make sense of what little remains ooh/ 'cause you left me with no love and no love to my name/ I'm still alive but I'm barely breathing/ just prayin' to a God that I don't believe in/ 'cause I got time while she got freedom/ 'cause when a heart breaks no it don't

break/ no it don't break, no it don't break even, no/ what am I gonna do when the best part of me was always you? And ----------'

"Yo?" Phenöm greeted, answering his S2 interrupting The Script's *Breakeven* ringtone, as he neared the Cutlass.

"Johnnie, where are you!?" Jackie asked, nearly in tears, calling Phenöm off of Jünior's iPhone which he had left in the house that day by accident.

"Jackie?"

"Yeah, where are you?"

"I'm in South Carolina right now, why what's up, where's Jünior?" he replied, lying about his whereabouts but needing to understand why Jackie was calling him from Jünior's phone.

"Nya just called me and told me that somebody told her that Mustafa was just escorted out of the school in handcuffs." Jackie informed him, as he opened the car's back door and grabbed the heavy duffel bag which sat on the backseat.

"Handcuffs!"

"I need to know what's going on but I got Ciara with me and I'm not taking my baby down to no police station."

"Aight, stay by the phone, let me call Tàbitha and see where she's at, she'll come get Ciara so that you can go check on bruh."

"Aight, hurry up and call me back."

"Aight." Phenöm returned, hanging up and banging his fist on the roof of the Cutlass before barking, "Shit!"

Phenöm dialed Tàbi's number as he walked back towards the house carrying the duffel bag, he was walking inside of the front door as Sharese *Tàbi* Hamelton answered the phone. He told her everything that Jackie had just told him and told her to go up to the house and get Ciara so that Jackie could go check on Jünior. Once Tàbi told him that she was on her way they disconnected the call, Phenöm climbed the flight of stairs of the 3-family house in route to the third floor. Phenöm leaned in and put his ear to the door so that he could hear what was going on within, when he was satisfied he took a step back and raised his right foot in the air.

With all of his strength Phenöm kicked the door in and stormed into the apartment already knowing where his target was hiding, he walked in on the 48-year old pot belly man who was trying to gather himself nervously. Phenöm walked over to him and aimed his gun in the guy's face telling him to get down on his knees, Phenöm sat the bag down on the floor and unzipped it before pulling out a roll of duct tape. He quickly duct taped the man's hands behind his back and then laid him across the bed, next he went into the bag and pulled out a Phillips head power drill.

"Please, you don't have to do this!" the guy whined, trying to see what Phenöm was doing.

"That's where you're wrong, I have to do this for my homie Paul, you faggot ass rapist!" Phenöm barked, walking up to the dudes head which was hanging off of the edge of the bed. "I'm goin' make sure that you don't put your hands on nann nother motherfucka in this lifetime, pussy!"

"Pl-pl-pl-pl-please, I'm b-b-b-beg y-y-y-yo-you, pleas..."

That was the last thing the guy was able to get out of his mouth before Phenöm began drilling into the back of his head with the drill, the guy screamed for a few moments before death consumed him. Phenöm wasn't here to play with him or waste time, he had to now find out what was going on with Jünior. Phenöm knew that he couldn't be out in the streets for too long knowing that he was on the run for murder. Once he was sure that the guy was dead he packed his things back up and walked out of the apartment like he never entered. Back to hillside he went!

11:57 a.m.
Green Street
▪ Newark ▪

"Mr. Mustafa Raheem, son of the famous kingpin Fahim, I guess the apple doesn't fall far from the tree does it?!" Ofc. Harvey said, sitting across from Jünior, whose hands were folded atop of the table in front of him with handcuffs on them. "I'm just curious, how could a piece of shit like yourself not have a rap sheet as far as the stretch marks on that dingy ass little drunk bitch that you call a mother!?"

Jünior squeezed his eyes to narrow slits while grilling Ofc. Harvey demonically, hands clenched into skin breaking tight fists, veins protruding violently, but he kept his mouth shut. Ofc. Perkins walked behind Jünior while saying, "Wayne, I don't think that you should bring Jackie Wilder up at a time like this, definitely not in the disrespectful manner that you're doing."

"Fuck that fucking alcoholic druggie bitch!"

"I said enough already!" Ofc. Perkins barked, trying to play the good cop in hopes that Jünior would bite.

"We've got a dead man downtown at the morgue and a young woman in the hospital fighting for her life," Ofc. Harvey spat, opening the yellow folder on the table in front of Jünior, showing him the crime scene photos. "And you're sitting here sympathizing with this piece of shit murderer!?"

"Not everyone is guilty, Wayne, you haven't even asked Mr. Raheem if he was there."

"Because I don't need to, I fucking know his ass was there!"

"Would you please interrogate the kid, rather than insult him?" Ofc. Perkins spat, turning his head towards Jünior. "Mustafa, tell my partner here that he's wrong, and that this is a huge mistake."

"Nah, he's right about two things, my mother is a drunk and ex-druggie," Jünior confirmed, still staring through Ofc. Harvey. "And, I was on Chadwick Avenue that day now that I think about it!"

"I knew it, you and Johnnie ---"

"However, I wasn't the shooter." Jünior said, cutting him off before he could finish his statement.

"If you weren't the shooter, then who was?" Ofc. Perkins questioned, believing that Jünior was foolish enough to fall for the good cop/ bad cop act.

"Lawyer."

"Speak up, boy, we can't hear you." Ofc. Harvey barked, leaning forward trying to hear what Jünior said.

"LAWYER!!!" Jünior yelled, leaning forward in his seat, nearly spitting in Ofc. Harvey's face as the word left his lips.

Jünior knew that there was no way hell that this interrogation was legit because he was a minor, from watching Law & Order SVU, Criminal Intent, and CSI Miami, he knew his rights as a minor. There was just no way that these two veteran Dt.s should have been questioning him without a lawyer and his mother present, even though they were just fishing for a lead. Of course Jünior knew that they didn't have anything on him to charge him with anything, they were barking up the wrong tree for real.

Jünior was sitting there wondering where Jackie was at because he had purposely told one of the students to tell Nya that he was being arrested. If his message was delivered to Nya he knew without a doubt that Nya had called Jackie, so there was no reason that Jackie wasn't down there right now. Jünior was beginning to get nervous about sitting there that long knowing that a few dudes had disappeared in police custody, the last thing he wanted was to die by the hands of the police.

The interrogation room was small and cramped with a stale smell of stillness, that lonely slit of air in the room peaked mountain tops. With so much tension compressed within, it felt nearly hard to breathe the longer that he sat there, to the point that color was slowly fading from Jünior's face. Ofc. Harvey and Ofc. Perkins couldn't believe that Jünior had just lawyered up on them without being able to trip him up over his own words convicting himself. Ofc. Harvey's face flipped down into a droopy sag, the hairs on the back of his neck stood up, his jaw tightened into a vise grip clench, releasing his fire spitting rage. Wiping his lips, Ofc. Harvey shook his head continuously while standing up, he was ready to charge Jünior with anything and just ship him to the youth house [Detention Center].

Jünior watched as both Dt.s walked out of the room leaving him sitting there with deep empty thoughts, not knowing what could happen next. Jünior wrapped his right hand around left fist and squeezed tightly, causing his knuckles to crack. As his nerves began to unravel completely, Jünior cracked the knuckles in his right hand with his left hand before standing up. Phenöm was somewhere hiding with every cop in Essex County looking for him and here Jünior was, down at the precinct being implicated, harassed, and pancaked with conspiracy, Jünior was in for a ride of all rides!

"Mr. Raheem, you are under arrest for possession of a weapon and resisting arrest." Sergeant Nunez informed, walking in with Lieutenant Ellen Microsoft, who looked like the actress Indira Varma, with Ofc. Harvey and Wright standing behind her in the hallway smiling.

"Weapon and resisting arrest?" Jünior questioned, hardly able to believe he was hearing what he was hearing. "You're kidding me right?"

"Hardly, now please stand up." Sergeant Nunez returned, standing over him with her handcuff keys in her hand.

"This is some bullshit!"

Tuesday February 13th, 2018

2:55 p.m.
15th Avenue
▪ Newark ▪

"*Time on my hands/ since you been away, boy/ I ain't got no plans/ no, no, no, no/ the sound of the rain/ against my window pane/ it's slow, it's slowly driving me insane, boy/ I'm going dow* ---" Nique sang loudly along with Mary J. Blige on her classic hit *I'm Going Down* as her *My Life* album softly melted throughout the alpine speakers of Nya's smoke gray Buick Lacrosse.

"Damn, bitch, it's only been a month, you need to get it together!" Nya said, while interrupting Nique's little *American Idol* moment, as she made a left turn off of 15th Avenue onto Camden Street.

"Whatever, Shenya, so what, I miss my bae, this month feels more like two years!"

"Nah, you're right, it has been mad different not having big head around," she returned, while looking at her rearview mirror eying Ciara and Monique sitting in the backseat asleep in their car seats. "Ciara has been asking for him like crazy."

"Yeah, it seems like Monique can feel Mustafa's absence also, she's been sitting at the front door with her jacket in her hand, holding the pink pony that Jünior won for her in Wildwood last year." Nique informed, as tears slowly stormed from her eyes rolling down her cheeks, balling her hands into tight fists.

"You know she's connected to him just as much as Ciara, Jünior's the only father that Monique's had since she was born." Nya said, making a right onto 14th Avenue, feeling her S2 vibrating under her right thigh.

Nya grabbed her phone with her left hand keeping her right hand on the steering wheel, she didn't have to look at the screen because she already knew who was assigned Avant's 4 Minutes ringtone. Nya handed Nique her phone, before saying, "It's Chämp, answer it."

"Hello?" Nique greeted, after swiping the touch screen to the right, answering the call and putting the phone on speaker.

"Yo, where's Nya?" Chämp replied ignorantly, already knowing that it was Nique answering the phone.

"I'm right here, what's up?"

"Who you in the car with?"

"Why?" she questioned, making a left onto Bergen Street after sitting at the red light for a few seconds.

"Because I need to holla at yo ass, why else!"

"Shut up, I'm with Nique and the babies."

"Aight, where y'all at?"

"Around, nigga, damn!" Nique spat, as Nya pulled up behind a gold Nissan Altima at the red light on Bergen Street and South Orange Avenue. "Why!"

"Mind your business, Nique." Chämp said, hearing the aggravation in her voice. "I'm on Munn and Central, I wanna know where y'all at cause I need to holla at both of y'all, it's important."

"Aight, meet us on 18th at the 99 Cent store." Nya told him, as the traffic started to move.

"Aight, I'll be there, how far away are y'all?"

"Damn, nigga, what are you the police or something with all of these damn location questions and shit!" Nique snapped jokingly.

"Give us like twenty minutes, we'll be right there."

"Aight, hurry up."

Nya had to laugh at how Chämp was coming on the phone lately. They had been talking behind everybody's back, trying to see where things would go. Nya definitely didn't want Jünior finding out that her and Chämp were kicking it. Jünior was so overprotective when it came to Nya, that she was afraid to confide in him about Chämp. Chämp had been feeling himself a lot more lately since Phenöm started hitting him with work [drugs]. Now Chämp had his little brother and his crew in Millville moving work for him. All of this was running through Chämp's mind as he prepared to get off the bus. He climbed off of the bus and walked into 99 Cent's parking lot.

"Yeah," Chämp said, answering his iPhone after hearing Freeway's *Free* ringtone. "Where are y'all at?"

"Pulling into the parking lot, we're in a ---"

"I see you, I see you." he told Nya, before she could finish her statement, watching Nya park two cars down from where he was standing.

Nya climbed out of her Lacrosse wearing a pair of all black Mauri's, a pair of tight fitted blue True Religion jeans, and a black Galaxy tank-top. She walked over to the 99 Cent store where Chämp was standing at, he had just gotten off of the number 24A bus just moments before Nya had pulled up. Chämp stood there in a pair of brown boot cut JCME jeans, a white, orange, and brown Polo button-up, a pair of tan construct Timbs, and a custom made brown Philadelphia Eagles fitted. As soon as Nya reached Chämp they embraced in a hug and said their greetings, then they peeled apart and began discussing why they had met up in the first place.

Nique sat in the car wondering what they were meeting Chämp here for, she needed to know what was so important that they had to come right now. She would've been right out there with them if the girls weren't in the backseat of the car, there was no way that she would ever leave her kids in a car alone. Even though Jünior was locked up, Nique knew that if he ever found out that she left Monique and Ciara in a car alone, he would flip his wig.

"So, what's up?" Nya asked, as a woman walked out of the 99 Cent store carrying two hands full of bags with her three children in tow.

"I just spoke to Jünior not too long ago, he wants to know how that other thing is coming along with Troy and Tàbi. He said that if everything is a go then y'all can move out on it."

"Ain't nobody doing shit until he gets home, and you can tell him that I said that."

"He said that you would say that, that's why he said to tell you to do as he say and not what you want." Chämp replied smiling, as 2 thick chicks walked into the 99 Cent store.

"We're not doing anything until his big head ass get out, we gotta get him out, so before we do anyth ---"

"He'll be home next week on house arrest until he goes back to court, but he expressed that he needs thing taken care of like yesterday."

"House arrest! House arrest for what, on what charges are they really charging him with!?"

"The conspiracy charges didn't stick but they hit him with resisting arrest and weapons charges." Chämp confessed, looking at Nya.

"What weapons! Jünior didn't have no fucking weapon when they came and locked him up at school!" she barked angrily.

"I know, look, it's all a bunch of bullshit to hold him until they find Phenöm or Jünior actually slips up and admits to a charge."

"Tell him that I said to call me, I don't know why he hasn't called me yet."

"I got you, just get on that other thing for him and I'll make sure that I tell him to call your phone."

"Aight, tell him to hold his head up in there, and let him know that I'm on the other thing." she said.

"Aight, hit me as soon as you find out the intel on that, let Troy know that he needs it done like yesterday." Chämp told her, giving her another hug before she departed.

"I'm about to go see Sofi."

"Okay, make sure you give Sofi my love, I know she could use it right about now."

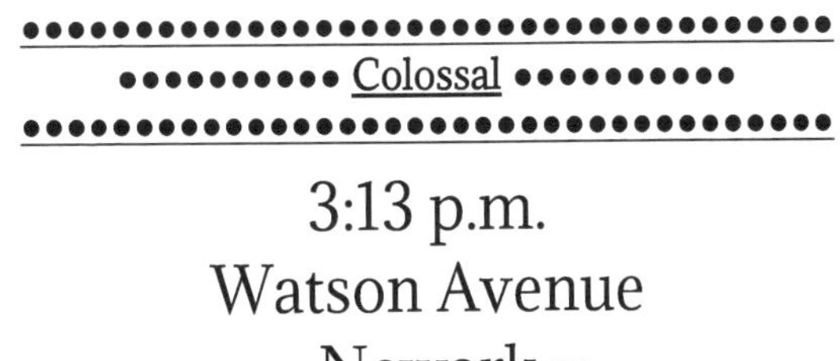

Colossal

3:13 p.m.
Watson Avenue
■ Newark ■

'Y'all take them shoes off your teeth/ stop runnin' your mouth/ no shoes, no feet, I'll run in your mouth/ I'll come to your house, me and my goons/ loadin' up bangers, ridin' under the moon/ throwin' up fingers sayin' "my side rule"/ if a nigga disagree, that's when my side prove/ that Maybach Coupe a cock-eyed fool/ and I'm "in it like Bennet" hoe, aren't I cool/ but if that thermostat switch and that needle move/ then the attitude switch and the heat'll move/ I got that, Shakita banana, clip for the tool ---------'

"Where the fuck is this nigga at?!" Dowe snapped, looking at the screen of his white iPhone 2S while sitting in his yellow Chevrolet Monte Carlo SS, listening to Lil Wayne's *Hit 'Em Up.*

"I don't know." his little brother answered, looking up towards Bergen as the number 39 bus pulled up to the bus stop on the corner.

"I know you don't know, dawg, I wasn't asking you where the nigga was at, I was just venting."

"Oh, aight."

Dowe had been sitting in his Monte Carlo which was parked on Watson Avenue directly across the street from Peshine Street School, facing Bergen in between Peshine and Hunterdon Street. He was on his way to his babymother's house to drop off his little brother, that's when he got a call for an ounce of weed. Besides driving his homie BigDeal around when he was doing his stick-ups, Dowe was a petty weed dealer but swore up and down that he was that nigga. Dowe ran around Newark lying about how much weed he sold and money that he made on a day to day basis, he thought people bought into his lies but he was only one that truly believed what he was saying.

Dowe was able to stay on his feet because his babymother would always give him her welfare check on the first of every month, he would take that check and flip it. Now he was good at selling weed and flipping that check every month but he couldn't save anything because he always blew his money on nonsense, after giving his babymother her money back. She would take that money and tend to the things that she had to tend to within her household, because Dowe lived at home with his mother still. When his babymother wouldn't give him her check because she was behind in certain bills, Dowe would cash in her food stamps for cash to make a quick flip, there was shame in Dowe's game. If he didn't do that he was out with his homies LilGuy and BigDeal robbing hustlers, a scheme that came back to bite them in the ass as of recently.

"I'm giving this nigga 5 more minutes and then I'm leaving." Dowe said, as a dude on a ten speed Huffy bike turned the corner off of Bergen.

"That must be him right there on that bike." Dowe's little brother announced, as Dowe's 2S began to ring.

"Nah, but this is him right here." he said, pointing down at his iPhone screen as the number flashed across it.

"Darrell!" his brother screamed, as Dowe was looking down at his phone's screen.

Hearing the urgency within his brother's voice as he screamed his real name, Dowe raised his head and looked in his brother's direction instead of ahead of them. Dowe's brother was in sheer shock, frozen stiff and scared shitless looking at the biker standing in front of the Monte Carlo, with a silencer equipped mach-11 aimed directly at the windshield. Dowe's eyes finally followed his brother's eyes which were full of tears, he was granted a split second of the view that his brother saw before both of their hearts dropped.

The biker squeezed tightly pulling the trigger of the mach-11 sending countless slugs into the driver side of the Monte Carlo, 2 bullets instantly smashing into Dowe's face, as glass debris quickly soaked the confines of the Monte Carlo. blood patterns splattered all over the interior of the Monte Carlo leaving a painted picture for police to see and clean up. Dowe's body was able to fall to the right covering his little brother's body, continuing to take a parade of bullets to his torso for good measure. The gunman stood on the bike with his finger on the trigger until the 30-round clip was empty, the nose of the mach-11 lighting up the night's hue sky. Cars driving by couldn't believe what was happening, right in front of Peshine Avenue School.

Once the clip was empty the gunman lowered the mach-11, grabbed the handlebars of the bike with his left hand, and began peddling his way into traffic. Because of the Goku Dragon Ball Z mask, the face of the gunman couldn't be seen as he rode across the street headed towards Hunterdon. Dowe's little brother lie underneath his body covered in blood, shaking fearfully after what had just happened but also because he had a bullet lunged into his left arm and right knee. People quickly climbed out of their cars when they were sure that the gunman was long gone, some had their phones out dialing 911, while some were filming the aftermath to post on Facebook, Instagram, and World Star HipHop.

A small crowd quickly formed around the Monte Carlo as speculators began to ask other speculators questions about what just happened, it wouldn't be long before the story was twisted into 10 different things that had taken place. All the while the gunman was riding up Custer Avenue now pedaling faster than he was originally, by the time he had crossed Chadwick Avenue he had ditched the bike and was power walking towards a stolen black 2009 Audi A4.

"Hurry up, nigga!" Ghoon barked, hanging out of the driver side window.

"Do you wanna be the next one to get shot, motherfucka?!" Phenöm replied, jogging around to the back door. "Y'all niggas must think its a game or something!"

Tuesday February 14th, 2018

2:55 p.m.

Doremus Avenue

■ Newark ■

"In another news update, the man shot to death in Newark yesterday on Watson Avenue has been identified as Darrell Clouds, the associate of Brandon Tymes, the man shot down last month on Chadwick Avenue. Both men have been rumored to have been involved in a string of robberies." news anchor, Pam Oliver, reported, staring into the news camera. *"Dt.s are trying to piece together the reasons for both deaths. Lead Dt. Sergeant Nunez has yet to give up any statements as where she stands with both murders, however---"*

"Yo, did you hear what the news said about that nigga Dowe?" Bennie asked, running into his cell interrupting Jünior as he was writing Nique a letter, listening to the news report airing on the TV outside of their cell.

"Yeah, I heard it, I told you I already knew who it was before the police knew who it was." Jünior replied, without looking up from the yellow notepad that he was writing on. "Once I find out what building that faggot ass nigga BigDeal in, he goin' get it too."

"I told you, I think the nigga is in lock up, my homie told me that the nigga was in building 3, but he popped off on somebody yesterday when he got off of the phone." Bennie informed. "He must've got the word about his brother getting killed last night, he probably figured he was next and wanted to go to lock-up instead of being around everybody else."

"Could be."

"What the fuck is you doing, nigga?"

"Nothing." Jünior answered, tearing the letter off of the pad and folding it up, he stuffed it into the envelope that was underneath the notepad.

"I know you ain't over there writing no letter and you only been in here for a couple of days!" Bennie clowned, looking over Jünior's shoulder trying to see what he was doing.

"I said I'm not doing nothing, why, what's up, bruh!?"

"I'm just saying ---"

"Don't just say shit, you do what you do and I'ma do what I do!" Jünior snapped, hating the fact Bennie was sitting there trying to mind his business. "You cool and everything but we ain't friends, we're locked up, this shit ain't summer camp!"

"Yeah, aight." Bennie returned, walking back out of the cell to get on the phone.

Jünior sat there in a green khaki county uniform with bobo's [knock off shoes] on his feet, he had been in the Essex County Jail which was call the Green Monster for about 5 weeks now. He didn't have a bail nor had he seen a public defender or a lawyer since he'd been there, Chämp had told him that he had spoken to a lawyer that was supposed to be getting him out on house arrest. However, Jünior had been sitting there waiting for this ghost of a lawyer which never came to see him, Jünior was getting angrier by the second. Jünior sealed up the letter by dipping his fingers in water and swiping it across the flap of the envelope.

He walked out of the cell and dropped it off at the Ofc.'s desk. Jünior then walked over to the phones and sat down, picking the phone up and dialing Chämp's number, he looked around the dayroom before getting comfortable. He had been waved up as an adult instead of being shipped to the Youth House, Jünior wasn't worried because he was going to hold his own no matter where he went to. The phone rang four times before Chämp answered the call, Jünior had to wait for the operator to give Chämp her spiel before connecting the call.

"Thank you for using Global Tel Link." the operator said, before Chämp greeted Jünior, "As salaamu alaikum wa rahmatullah, Ahki."

"Wa alaikum as salaam wa rahmatullah wa barrakatu, Ahki, what do you got for me?" Jünior asked, getting right down to it.

"I spoke to a brother down at the Masjid and the brother gave me the number to a lawyer that he said is winning right now, he said that he could get you off." Chämp informed, hoping that this news would bring light to Jünior's dark situation.

"Well, why hasn't he been down here to see me, to tell me something, anything!"

"I had to get the money that he was asking for, he wanted $1,500.00 upfront as a retainer's fee, so I had to take the money that Doug and them were putting up for Phenöm and give it to him."

"Aight, so again, where the fuck is he?"

"He should be coming to see you...what's today," Chämp asked, not looking for an answer as he thought about the day of the week. "He'll be down there tomorrow, his name is James Flanory."

"James Flanory!"

"Hey, you know him?"

"Hell no, but his name sounds like he was raised right there on Chadwick Avenue with 7re and them!"

"Look, beggars can't be choosy, we're working with what we can so deal with it, now he says that he can get you out on house arrest, so be thankful that you'll be home sooner than later." Chämp snapped.

"Yeah, aight, did you tell Shenya what I said?"

"Yeah, and she said to tell you she ain't doing shit until you come home, I told her what you said but she has her mind made up already and she's not budging."

"Aight, good looking, you did your thing, bruh."

"Nya also said to tell you to call her phone, she doesn't understand why you haven't been called her."

"Aight, I'ma call her right now, good looking out, bruh, shakran [thank you], as salaamu alaikum wa rahmatullah."

"You got it, afkran [you're welcome], my boy, wa alaikum as salaam wa rahmatullah wa barrakatu."

12:45 p.m.
Farley Avenue
▪ Newark ▪

"Nom, how is Sofi doing?" Mir asked, once Phenöm had locked the door behind him after just coming from the hospital.

"She's still in a coma, doctors said it all on her if she wakes up or not."

"I know them bills is high as hell!" Jackie joined in, calling out from the living room.

"Huh?" Phenöm gasped, making sure he heard his aunt correctly.

"Keeping her up in that hospital ain't cheap, shit, a gotdamn broken finger goin' run yo ass in the hole for the rest of your life, fuckin' with U.M.D.'s ass!"

"You right, Jack, but now ain't the time for that." Lee jumped in, seeing her son's face as Jackie spoke. "You really need to work on your timin'."

"Her bills are good, we keep them up to par." Phenöm returned, as he turned to walk away as his phone started ringing. "Hello?"

"Yo, what's good lil nigga?" Havok greeted, smiling at the sound of a familiar voice.

"Who the fuck is this? Mari?"

"Yeah, nigga, fuck is you sayin' my shit over the phone like that?"

"Nigga please, if you don't get your college going ass outta here!" Phenöm clowned, knowing how Havok really got down.

"Yeah aight, nigga, what's good with you though? How's Sofi doing? I heard what happened, that shit is wild." Havok said, having got the news as soon as it happened.

"She good, I just came from seeing her."

"That's what's up." he said, wishing he was home to do something about Sofi getting shot because she'd always been solid with him. "Yo, I need you to do me a favor."

"No shit!" Phenöm shot back, already knowing that when Havok called.

"Shut yo ass up and listen, you know it's only a few people I trust like that, and yo goofy ass just happens to be one of them."

"Lucky me". he returned, being as sarcastic as he could.

"Seriously though, I need you to hit bruh for me and see what's up with that movement." Havok said, wanting Phenöm to reach out to 1090.

"Would if I could, but bruh cuffed right now, and I don't have his number."

"Fuck!" Havok gasped, needing to get with 1090 or Capo so that he could get some more ecstasy pills. "Aight, see what you can do and get back with me."

"I got you, skoob."

"Another thing, you still sharp with it?"

"Fuck you talkin' 'bout, I keep it on me, and I always hit when I pull it out."

"That's good, that's good, I may need you in the near future."

"Yeah aight, get off my line so I can get ready to take my bitch out for Valentine's Day." Phenöm told him as he read Cynt's text that had come through on his phone.

Cynt 1:09 p.m.
So I guess I have to cater
to myself for Valentine's Day !!!

"You funny ass hell, tell wifey I said what up."

"You still there?" Phenöm clowned, debating whether or not he should text her back. "I thought I told yo ass to beat your feet and skedaddle."

"Boy, yo ass lucky I can't get to yo punk ass." Havok laughed, as his roommate walked into their dorm room with his bestfriend.

"Yeah aight, fuck you goin' do, give me the notes to your next exam?!" Phenöm countered, knowing just how to get under Havok's skin as he texted Cynt back.

"Oh, yo ass full of mothfuckin' jokes today, huh?"

Phenöm 1:13 p.m.
I'm on my way to get you now so be ready

"Aye, what can I say, your sorrows are my jokes."

"You know what?" Havok replied, looking over at his roommate who was pulling his bong out to smoke with his bestfriend. "I'ma let you get that so that you can feel better, but I come home I'm fuckin' you up, just know that."

"Yeah, yeah, yeah, I'm sweating in my boots!"

"Yeah aight, get up with me and let me know what's what."

"Say less, I got you."

"Good looks."

"No doubt, one.

"One."

Life in its rare form was fucking up Phenöm up big time, especially since Jünior was locked up. Chämp was back and forth from Newark to Millville, even though he wasn't comfortable without Jünior around. Phenöm knew that he had to keep trucking, just because Jünior was boxed in, didn't mean the show stopped. That was something that him and Jünior had in common.

Tuesday February 18th, 2018

3:15 p.m.
Vailsburg Terrace
■ Newark ■

"Ken, what's up, cuz?" Boyn greeted, sitting in the passenger seat of a red Mercedes Benz S550.

"Same ole shit, tryna get to this dollar." Ken replied, standing on the deadend side of Vailsburg Terrace just off of Myrtle Avenue, along with his little crew.

"That's what I like to hear, how much you got for me?" Boyn asked, taking a quick look around the block.

"I ain't got shit for you," Ken shot back jokingly, standing there looking towards the corner for fiends or even the police. "The real question is what do you got for me?"

"You know me, if you got the money, I got what you need." Boyn confessed, as Sames handed him a blunt of sour diesel.

"I'm good right now, but if you run across some fire dope, hit my phone."

"Kay, let me get change for a ten." his brother Bru said, standing on their porch with two fiends.

"I don't got it."

"Where's Fitz?" Boyn asked, looking around the block.

"He where he at, I don't keep track of no man." Ken shot back, hating when Boyn came looking for Fitz.

"Yeah aight, when you see him, let him know that I'm looking for him." he said, passing the blunt back to Sames, whom was in the driver's seat of the S550.

"Nah, you can call his phone and let him know that you're looking for him yourself, I don't work for the post office!"

"Yo, your mouth is goin' get you in some shit that your ass can't get you out of." Boyn said, wanting to get out and address Ken's snappy mannerism.

Ken pulled his shirt up exposing him .9mm, before saying, "Trust me, I ain't worried about shit, you better go try that shit on them niggas down the hill, nigga. You forgot that I know you!"

"Yeah aight, you make sure that you keep that on you at all times."

"Trust me, if you catch me without it, you got every right to knock my shit off." Ken smirked, lowering his shirt back down.

"Oh, I will!" he reassured, smiling devilishly.

"Be my guest."

"Yeah aight, make sure you tell my aunt that I said what's up."

"I got you."

Boyn rolled his window up as Sames pulled away from the curb slowly. Boyn always came up here to check on his little cousins, it was something he did daily. With the death of Dowe, Boyn wanted to come check on his family to make sure that they were on point. Boyn was looking for Fitz because that was his little brother. Tito *Boyn* Travis was born and raised in the Vailsburg section of Newark. Though he was well known for putting his gun game down, those that knew him knew that he was all mouth. Boyn couldn't fight for shit and he never tried to make himself out to be no fighter. He just knew how to surround himself with the right people, thrusting himself to the top of the food chain.

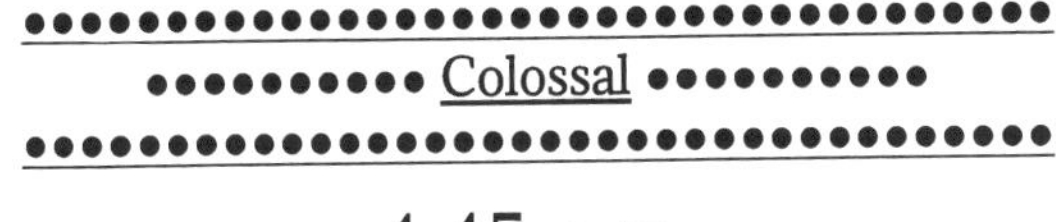

4:45 p.m.
Madison Avenue
■ Newark ■

"Jackie, where is Ciara's clean clothes at?" Nique yelled from Jünior's room, as she dug through all of the clothes that were piled up in the corner.

"I don't know, I think Shenya came and got them yesterday thinking that they were her dirty clothes." Jackie answered, sitting in the living room drinking a Lime A Rita, watching *The Wendy Williams Show*.

"So, she has no clean clothes here at all?"

"Elizabeth, I don't fucking know, go look in my room she might have something in there!" Jackie snapped.

"Aight."

Nique walked out of Jünior's room and headed down the hall towards Jackie's room, she hated coming to Jackie's house when Jünior wasn't around because Jackie's mouth could get reckless. Though Jackie didn't have anything against Nique, she just hadn't been much of a people's person ever since Fahim had gotten arrested. No matter what a person said or did to or for her, Jackie just wasn't into doing much smiling unless Ciara was the cause.

Nique walked into Jackie's room and started looking around for any of Ciara's clothes, as soon as she stepped in front of the dresser she spotted a letter addressed to her from Jünior. She picked the letter up to see if it had been opened, once she saw that Jackie hadn't open the letter she walked back out of the room and headed straight to the living room. Jackie was sitting there laughing at Wendy Williams who was going in on a group of celebrities and their outfits, Nique stepped right into the room and stood in front of Jackie's way.

"Why didn't you tell me that Mustafa wrote me?!"

"Because I had better things to do, now get your lil funky ass from in front of my TV before I be in a jail cell right next to him for killing your ass for blocking my show!"

"How long ago did this letter come?"

"Girl, I don't know, look at the damn envelope and get the fuck outta my way!" she yelled, shoving Nique to the right.

"Whatever, the next time that he writes me, make sure I get the letter or I'm goin' break that dumbass TV and then you won't be so busy." Nique barked, walking off with much attitude as she ripped open the letter, and began to read it.

Nique, *2/15/18*

As salaamu alaikum, Nique. I miss you so much, I never thought that it was possible to miss someone that doesn't belong to you, the way that I miss you! Word is bond, these past couple of months have felt like eternities away from you and my babies, this is a feeling that I could never get used to. The niggas in here are clowns, they think being in here is like some sort of badge of honor and shit. SMH!!! They got me bunking with this kid named Bennie, he's from Lyons Avenue and Clinton Place.

For the most part he's a cool dude, the only thing that bothers me about him is he's blood so a lot of his homies be in and out of my cell. You know I ain't with that wack ass blood shit, so when they come in I step out just trying to keep my distance from people. I've been offering salat five times a day as I should and making sure that I ask, Allah, for his mercy in this situation. I've been heavy in my Qu'ran and when I'm not studying, I'm reading a hood novel. They have so many hood novels in here it's ridiculous, shit, maybe these niggas come back for the hood stories! LOL!!!

I just got my hands on this book by the Ahki, Tweek SOB, the title of the book is Young And Reckless. It's a short story but so far it's a good read, the brother has a gift for real. I know him from the seeing him around town and I used to drop work off to him years ago, but I never knew that he could write like that, he's talented.

How are my babies doing? Please kiss them for me, I miss them so much that words could never truly express the way my soul has been calling for them. I miss sitting in my room watching them try to play the game, claiming that the other one is cheating. I miss hearing their voices. I miss their touches. I miss waking up to their smiles. I just miss my babies, all three of y'all!

Chämp keeps telling me that I'm coming home so I might be home when you receive this letter, shit, I hope that I am! But if I'm not home by the time you get this, just know that I miss you and can't wait to feel your touch. Your ass better not be out there fucking with no other niggas either, I don't wanna hear that 'I love you' shit. Bitches cheat on their nigga while he's home so miss me with all of that shit, if I find out that you even out there holding conversations with niggas.

I swear on Ciara's life I'm done with you! I know that this can be an adventure on you with me being gone, but I promise you that I'm coming home sooner than later, just bare with me, Nique. I love you, baby, I've been thinking a lot about us and I think that I'm ready to make it official, maybe. You know how I feel about relationships, I don't feel like a woman can be faithful to a nigga especially when I don't even have my shit all the way together. As a Muslim man I know that it's my job to take care of my family, so that's what I'm trying to do before I commit to anything as far as we go.

I'm trying to make it through this whole ordeal without stressing and that's why I haven't called you or Shenya, I know that by me hearing y'all's voice I'm goin' go through it more than what I already am. So please understand why I haven't called y'all yet, this whole thing is really taking a toll on me, but I'm masking my own pain extremely well.

On to another note, how is Sofi doing? Is there any progress in her condition? What is the doctor talking? Has that Dt. called you since I've been gone? If so, what is he talking about? Did he ask anything about me? Don't tell that motherfucka shit, baby, just leave everything up to me, I got it, that's my word, wallahi. I love you, Nique, I can't wait to get out of here and feel your lips against mine, I miss the way those big ass lips feel wrapped around this dick. LOL!!!!! Nah, for real though, I miss you, baby, you know you mean the world to me, right? Let me go, my cellie just walked in the room. I hope you got to see the news today, I told you I got things under control, I love you, kiss my babies for me.

Love,

-

Jünior-

"Damn, I love the shit outta this nigga!" Nique thought to herself, folding the letter back up as tears slowly rolled down her cheeks.

Tuesday February 25th, 2018

6:19 p.m.

Peshine Avenue

■ Newark ■

"Mmmmmm, mmmmmm!"

"What did you say?" Phenöm asked, standing next to the 3-foot hole that he'd just dug up.

"Mmmmm, mmmmmmm, mmmm!"

Snatching the tape off of the man's mouth that was lying on the ground tied up, Phenöm replied, "What the fuck are you talking about?"

"Come on, Johnnie, don't do this, son!" the guy begged, arms tied behind his back with his legs tied together at the ankles. "On everything, I don't know nothing about what happened to your brother."

"I beg to differ, see what we have right now is a failure to communicate, I know that you were there when my brother was raped!"

"I didn't want to do that to him, I was forced to do that shit, trust me," he whined, trying to figure a way out of the mess that he was in. "I didn't want to be there, he held me against my will, I swear!"

"Now, how can I trust you when you first said that you didn't have nothing to do with it, but switched your statement and said that you were held against your free will," Phenöm said, pulling a water hose from next to the house that they were behind. "Answer me that."

"Please, Johnnie, I swear, I won't say anything to anybody about this, just let me go."

"Oh, I'm not worried about that, you won't see the light of day to be able to say a word let alone discuss this matter." he replied, sitting the hose down and pulling the duck tape back out of his back pocket.

"Come on, man, do fucking do this shit!"

"Nigga, shut up!" he barked, punching the guy in his mouth with brute force.

Phenöm ripped a nice size piece of tape off of the roll, and then grabbed the water hose and stuffed it into the guy's mouth. The guy was still a little dazed from the punch but he was trying to keep Phenöm from putting the hose into his mouth, so Phenöm began punching him in his face wildly until the man was unresponsive. Phenöm stuffed the end of the hose in his mouth and taped it in there by wrapping the tape around his head about seven times, making sure to not cover his nose. Once the hose was secure Phenöm dragged the guy towards the hole that he had just dug up and tossed his body inside of it leaving his head sticking out, and then he began to toss the dirt back in the hole.

Phenöm walked over to the house and turned the water on before walking away, he didn't even bother to sit there and watch the guy drown. The guy woke up as the water started running into his mouth, he was choking fast, he couldn't swallow enough water fast enough. His eyes darted towards Phenöm's back as he walked into the darkness. Phenöm let out a little chuckle as he heard the guy struggling to breath, he made his exit with his mind now on finding a way to get at BigDeal who was still in the Green Monster.

•••••••••••••••••••••••••••••••••

●●●●●●●●●● Colossal ●●●●●●●●●●
●●●●●●●●●●●●●●●●●●●●●●●●●●●●●●●●●●

8:21 p.m.
Farley Avenue
■ Newark ■

"Shit, girl, gotdamn!" Jünior moaned, with his head tilted back, eyes closed, toes digging into the soles of his black mid-top Air Forces, and his hands gripped tightly around Nique's slim 23" waist. She hungrily gyrated her hips suffocating her pussy with Jünior's dick, riding him reverse cowgirl style.

Jünior had missed his replica of the beautiful singer Keyshia Cole, he loved that fact that Nique's facial features mirrored every curve of Keyshia Cole's. Nique even had the gap in between her two front teeth in which Keyshia Cole once had before getting fixed, Jünior found that gap to be extremely sexy on Nique. Nique stood 4'10" with a butter pecan skin complexion, long jet brown hair that naturally hung down to the mid drift of her back. At 17-years of age Nique's body was amazingly cloning to Lafayette, Louisiana's own lovely native model Bri E. aka Ms. Ma'am, Bri E at 130lbs. Nique was half African American, half Brazilian, and Caucasian, her father was African American and her mother was half Caucasian and half Brazilian.

"Ooh, daddy, r-r-right, r-right th-there," Nique moaned out excitedly, with her hands on Jünior's knees, her legs folded in half one on each side of Jünior's, knees on the edge of his bed, head turned around towards Jünior. Stiff nippled titties bouncing slightly, as she methodically arched her back, enticingly raising her pussy up and down on Jünior's murderously erect 9-inches. "P-p-pl-pl-please....ooohh shit, m-m-motherfucka, pl-please don't s-s-stop!!"

"I missed this pussy so fucking much!" Jünior admitted, sucking on his bottom lip, feeling the vise grip of Nique's vaginal walls contracting viciously around his dick.

"Ooh, I know y-y-you did," Nique replied, closing her eyes while licking her lips seductively, as her warm nectar cover Jünior's dick like a coat of liquid skin. "I kept it nice and...ooohh....I kept it nice and tight for you, bae, gotdamn, boy, you feel so fucking good in this pussy!"

Nique was wetter than she'd ever been since fucking with Jünior, it was always wet but after not seeing him or feeling his touch for over 2 months, her body was yearning for him fiendishly. Nique was putting a hurting on the dick forcing Jünior to play nice in the pussy to keep from cumming quick, he wanted to lavish distantly inside of the confines of the walls that he miss dearly. However, when Nique leaned forward and grabbed her ankles Jünior completely lost his mind, he couldn't fathom the feeling that engulfed Jünior's being. Nique's pussy had opened up just enough to suck Jünior's dick in whole as she braced herself for the pleasing pain to come, Jünior hungrily slid seven inches inside of Nique wrapping his head around her g-spot causing her toes to curl.

Without lifting her body an inch Nique grinded steadily and slowly on the dick giving them both unquestioned pleasure, in West Indian style swirls, while rubbing her clit [clitoris] against the length of Jünior's thick vein popping shaft. She could feel the head of Jünior's dick throbbing with pulsating blood rushing force, so she spread her ass cheeks wide, lifted her body up just slightly, and jammed her pussy back down onto Jünior's dick. It was the right pressure needed to burst Jünior's pipes, Jünior sat up and wrapped his arms around Nique's waist and gripped her in an intense and passionate bear hug.

"What the fuck!" Jünior growled, preparing to pull his dick out of Nique"s pussy and paint the top of her ass cheeks with his semen.

"Uh-uh!" Nique yelled, forcing her pussy back down onto his dick, still swirling her hips hungrily. "I want you to cum in your pussy, daddy!"

"N-N-Nique ---"

"Cum in your pussy, bae, I need to feel all of you inside of me." she seductively whined, tightening her vaginal walls even tighter around his dick in a suction manner. "Cum in your pussy, boy."

"Nique, w-w-w-wwe.......shit," Jünior moaned, as the avalanche began, causing him to pump harder into the belly of Nique's pussy, tightening his grip around her. "Aaggghhhh!"

Now it was Nique's turn to bite down on her bottom lip as Jünior's warm semen filled her insides, mixing in with her flavorful nectar. Although Nique didn't get to cum she was so very content right at that moment, all she needed right then was to see the smile on Jünior's face that she was gazing at. The whole time that Jünior was locked up Nique blamed herself for him being in there, with all of the murders that were happening as of late Nique had no real idea as of what she'd pushed him into doing.

To see that BigDeal's little brother was murdered just days after BigDeal was locked up, Nique knew without a doubt that Phenöm did it and Jünior gave the order from jail. Nique had screamed at Jünior that night in the cemetery telling him to kill in the name of her sister, and that's what he was doing. Now Nique didn't know how far Jünior was planning on going with this whole thing because bodies were still popping up everywhere around them, people that she found herself knowing in one way or another.

Lying back on his bed, chest heaving up and down from his heavy breathing, Jünior said, "I can't believe you just.....yo, I cannot believe that we just did that! What now? What if you really get pregnant?"

"If I get pregnant Ciara and Monique is goin' have a brother or sister!" Nique replied seriously, spinning around on Jünior's semi-erect dick without releasing him from her pussy. She laid down on top of him, pressing her head against his chest, the crown of her head right underneath the cradle of his chin. "Mustafa, I've been thinking tha ---"

"Thinking is a good thing, thinking is the master key to success." he told her, while running his right hand through her sweaty hair.

"I'm serious, bae, these last 6 weeks were hell on me and Monique, not just Ciara."

"I know, me being away from the 3 of y'all is what hurt me the most, not being able to see y'all faces was the end to all beginnings." he confessed, looking deep into Nique's eyes.

"Jünior, I want you to move in with us, you and Ciara," Nique blurted out, after lifting her head off of his chest. "Monique needs you there in her life every day, every morning, every night, she needs her lil sister with her 24/7, 365."

"Dominique Perez, are you asking me to be your boyfriend?" Jünior smiled, looking at Nique, seeing the urgency within her eyes.

"Yes, nigga, I am!"

"And, you're really serious about this?"

"What do you think?"

"I can be a handful, Nique, you sure this is what you want?"

"Nigga, I just let you cum inside of me, yes, I'm serious and sure that this is what I want and need."

"Yeah, you did just let a nigga bust all in that wet shit."

"Well?"

"Nique, I've been your boyfriend for almost 3 years now, I wouldn't have it any other way."

"I know that already, but am I your girlfriend, are you goin' let the world know that I'm yours?"

"Now you know that all of this shit is mine, girl!" Jünior shot back, grabbing Nique's ass cheeks with both of his hands, squeezing each check playfully.

"Yeah, aight, you better start claiming me and not just Monique as yours, or somebody else just might be getting a taste of all of this tight wet pussy!" Nique said, squeezing her vaginal walls around his dick, causing his dick to began to come back to life.

"Yeah, aight, don't fucking pay with me Nique, I'll be back in the fucking Monster for murder one for real this time!"

"So then you're going to move in with us?"

Jünior let her ass go and wrapped his arms around her body, then looked up to the ceiling, before saying, "Let me think about it for a few days."

Tuesday February 28th, 2018

4:57 a.m.

16th Street

▪ Newark ▪

"So, your source said that he's in there?" asked Ofc. Harvey, as he sat in the passenger seat of the unmarked burgundy GMC Envoy LS, equipped with the Hemi.

"It's only one way to find out." Ofc. Perkins returned, picking up the police radio that was sitting on his lap, as he sat in the driver's seat of the Envoy. "All units move in, and remember that the suspect is armed and dangerous."

The morning was innocently still and quiet on 16th Street and 19th Avenue, the sun had yet to set and the birds had yet to sing. Ofc. Perkins had received some information from a source who was suppose to have seen Phenöm enter the apartment building in the middle of the block, this was the tip that they were looking for. There were three unmarked vehicles scattered throughout the block and three more on the block over just in case Phenöm tried to make a run for it.

Officer Dwayne Harvey stepped out of the Envoy standing 6'2", weighing 180lbs., he was wearing a pair of black Wrangler jeans, a black JCME T-shirt, and a pair of steel toe Payless boots. Officer Erik Perkins climbed out of the SUV standing 5'9", weighing 210lbs., he was wearing a pair of blue JCME jeans, a dark grey PePe T-shirt, and a pair of black on black Columbia boots. Both Dt.s were wearing nickel plated steel Teflon bullet proof vest, with their police badges swinging around their necks.

"All units in position." Ofc. Perkins ordered into his radio, standing beside the Envoy holding his 11-shot chrome black .40 caliber at his side.

"I bet you he never thought that we would find his ass here!" laughed Ofc. Harvey as Ofc. Strauss, Ofc. Hall, Ofc. Allen, Ofc. Hollstead, Ofc. Brandt, and Ofc. Peters surrounded the 4-story building from front to back.

"All units in place, Dt.." said the Ofc., standing near the front door, holding his radio to his mouth.

"Copy that." Ofc. Perkins returned, looking over at Ofc. Harvey before proceeding towards the house quickly, turning his head towards his partner to respond to his statement. "Yeah, but I bet you his ass be shocked when he sees all of these guns we brought for his ass!"

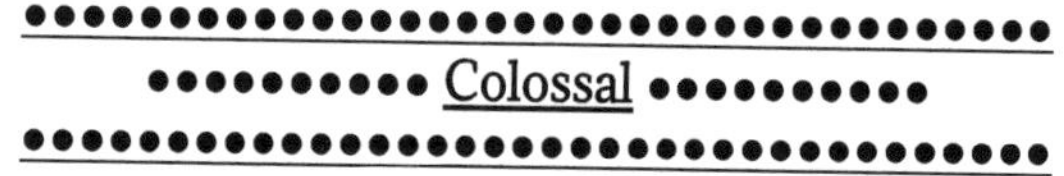

'Is my mind playing tricks, like Scarface and Bushwick/ Willie D, having nightmares of girls killing me/ she mad because what we had didn't last/ I'm glad because her cousin let me hit the ass/ fuck the past, let's dwell on the 500SL, the E&J and ginger ale..........'

"How many more nights are you going to be out there doing, God, knows what, while my dumb ass is sitting here wondering if you're dead or cornered off by the fucking police!" Cynt questioned, as she stood in the bathroom doorway, while the Notorious B.I.G.'s *One More Chance* played loudly on her sound system in the living room.

"What's the matter, you worried about a nigga?" Phenöm returned, smiling while scrubbing his skin roughly with the soapy green wash rag, as he stood in the shower looking at Cynt.

"No, I just like staying up until 6 in the morning, knowing that I have work in the a few hours!" she snapped, standing there with both of her hands on her hips.

"Well, in my defense, it's Saturday and you don't have to be to work until noon, plus it's not 6 o' clock, it's only like 5:15 if that."

"That's not the fucking point, Johnnie!"

"Yeah, well, get to the point already," he told her, turning his back so that he could rinse the soap off. "I'm tryna enjoy my fucking shower!"

"The fucking point is your stupid ass is wanted for murder and you're out there in the streets like you can't be fucking seen!"

"Why don't you just go ahead and dial the crime stoppers hotline and tell them where the the fuck I'm at!"

"Don't be fucking dumb, why the fuck would I do some stupid shit like that!?"

"You might as well, you standing there screaming that I'm wanted for a fucking body like these dumb ass walls ain't thin as shit!"

"Boy, please, can't nobody hear me through these walls with that shower running." Cynt replied, just seconds before they both heard a knock at the front door.

Phenöm and Cynt both froze as they looked at one another after hearing the knocking at the door, both of their heart rates quickly shot through the roof. As Phenöm looked around the bathroom he realized that he'd left his gun in the bedroom, he had to make it to his gun before Cynt answered the door. Phenöm had promised himself that when the time came he was going to out just like Larry Davis. Larry Davis a.k.a. Adam Abdul-Hakeem, was Phenöm's idol and hero, he was and still is the only gangster to shoot it out with the NYPD [New York Police Department] in a project apartment and get away with it.

The man not only terrorized the streets but he single handedly took on the NYPD, both on the street and in the courtroom. He shot it several police in a shootout and then turned around and beat the charge in court! Phenöm may have looked like the talented rapper by the name of Ransom from Jersey City, New Jersey, but he wanted to be just like Larry Davis.

As Phenöm turned the shower water off, Cynt walked out of the bathroom in pursuit to answer the door, she didn't know what to expect at 5:20 in the morning other than the police. Phenöm had quickly climbed out of the shower and rushed into the bedroom, where he first went to grab his gun before reaching for a pair of jeans. The idea was for him to lay low until Jünior could get him a lawyer to walk him in for questioning, but then the money they had for him had to go to Jünior so that he could get out of jail.

Still, Jünior had told Phenöm that he had the plans in motion to get Phenöm the best defense lawyer, and Phenöm knew that he would because his brother had yet to let him down. Phenöm had been staying at his girlfriend Cynt's apartment, because somehow or another police found out that he was crashing at his cousin's house in Hillside. It was getting harder and harder to hide out because he kept going out at night to either make money or put in some work, so his face was still being seen throughout the streets.

Standing at the bedroom door peeking his head out looking towards the front door, he pulled the hammer back on his .38 revolver to make sure he was ready. Cynt reached the front door and looked out of the peephole but she couldn't see anything, there were two shadowy figures stand afar but the darkness of the hallway made it hard to see. She slowly put her hands on the door and with a nervous pitch in her voice, she asked, "Who is it?"

"It's Newark Police, ma'am, we have a search warrant, please open up the door." Ofc. Harvey replied, holding the search warrant up to the peephole. "We have reason to believe that you are housing a murder suspect in your house."

"I'm sorry but there's no person in here wanted for no such crime." she returned.

"Please open up the door or we will be forced to kick it in."

"I'm not opening a damn thing for you or nobody else!"

"Ms., we have a warrant which states that you have to let us inside of the premises, just open the do ---"

"I don't give a fuck if you had Barack Obama and Hillary Clinton with you, I'm not opening my motherfucking door for nothing!"

"Okay," Ofc. Perkins responded calmly, turning towards Ofc. Strauss, Ofc. Hall, Ofc. Allen, Ofc. Hollstead, Ofc.

Brandt, and Ofc. Peters who were hiding on the steps holding a batting ram. "Kick it in."

The Ofc.s quickly climbed the stairs positioning themselves directly in front of the door, they were trained for situations just as such. The hallway was rather small, dark, and burned with the scent of piss, liquor, and weed smoke, your average smelling hallway in the ghetto. It was extremely stuffy within and the smoke detectors kept squeaking every 3 minutes, the situation was one of many in which the Ofc.s invaded hallways such as these. Ofc. Harvey and Ofc. Perkins both stepped to the side with their guns held high aimed at chest level, prepared to shoot if necessary.

Ofc. Strauss and Ofc. Hall raised the batting ram high in the air gripping it tightly. Ofc. Allen and Ofc. Hollstead assisted in the measuring of the ram with the locks. Ofc. Perkins held up his left hand raising three fingers and began to count down, he did this without speaking a word verbally. Once his three fingers had come down forming a solid fist, he nodded his head giving the go ahead signal. The Ofc.s swung the batting ram backwards and with the momentum of their bodies, they swung the ram into the doorknob and locks. The force from the batting ram not only forced the door open but it took the entire door off of the hinges, taking the frame along with it.

"What the fuck!" Cynt screamed angrily, as her door came flying open.

"My bad, sis, where's Johnnie?" Doug laughed, stepping into the apartment after shoving her way in forcefully, with Chämp in tow.

"Why are y'all playing so damn much!"

"We thought it was Johnnie behind the door trying to act like you." Chämp answered, closing the door behind himself.

"Where is he at anyway?"

"He's in the bathro ---"

"I'm right here, what's good?" Phenöm answered, cutting Cynt off as he stepped into the living room with his .38 in his right hand.

"Who did you think was at the door?" Chämp asked, spotting the gun in Phenöm's hand.

"Y'all knocking on the door and barging in this motherfucka at 5 in the morning like y'all the fucking police, who do you think we thought was at the door?" Cynt shot back, taking a seat on her couch as her heart rate began to slow down.

"My bad." Doug told her, seeing how nervous Cynt looked.

"Shit, the whole fucking building heard y'all."

"We said our bad, nigga, damn." Chämp snapped, looking at Phenöm, challenging him with his eyes.

"What the fuck do y'all want anyway?"

"Jünior said that it's going down tonight and he needs you to be on point cause Tàbi's not going no more, it's me, you, and Chämp." Doug answered, as Cynt stared at the trio as if they were all crazy.

"Chämp!?"

"Yeah, me, nigga, you got a problem with that?"

"You ain't bout this life, this ain't scrabble, nigga!"

"Fuck you, Phenöm."

"Sensitive ass nigga," Phenöm barked, turning around to walk back into the bedroom. "Tell Jünior to call me, this ain't goin' work."

"Whatever." Doug replied, looking from Phenöm to Chämp, shaking her head at how they treated one another from time to time.

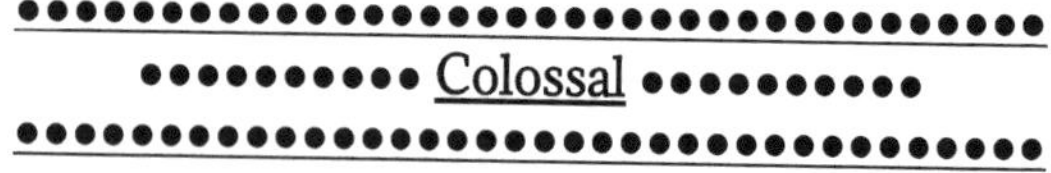

After searching the entire building from top to bottom Ofc. Harvey was full of anger and rage, he looked towards his partner and shook his head from left to right. He wasn't just mad because Phenöm wasn't in the apartment, his partner had taken them on a wild goose chase and now they owed this woman for knocking her door off of the hinges. She could go down to City Hall and make the biggest complaint against them, not only was Phenöm not in there but there was no traces of him ever being there! Ofc. Perkins's source had them chasing ghost and looking like idiots in front of their entire team, so far all that they had learned today was what not to do, they stood off to side laughing at Ofc. Harvey and Ofc. Perkins.

The team was back to square one on finding Phenöm, he was clever enough to not be anywhere that they had been searching. Ofc. Harvey had to really sit back and try and figure out where to go next, they had a killer on the loose and bodies were continuously piling up every day. Ofc. Perkins was ready to hunt down his source and see where they had gotten this information from, he was so pissed that they had run into a brick wall because of his sources.

Tuesday March 16th, 2018

12:02 a.m.

Doremus Avenue

■ Newark ■

"Butler, pack it up, you made bail." corrections Ofc. Browards announced, after popping the locks on BigDeal's cell door.

"Oh shit, nigga, you outta here." Jetter said, hopping up to see what BigDeal was gonna leave him.

BigDeal got up and walked to the cell door, and asked, "You sure I made bail?"

"Yo name Tramis Butler, right?" the C.O. asked, Ofc. Browards returned, standing at the Ofc.'s desk waiting for BigDeal to step out.

"Yeah, that's me."

"Well then pack yo shit and let's go, nigga, you made bail."

"Aight, here I come."

"Hurry the fuck up!" Ofc. Browards shot back, happy to see BigDeal get off his tier.

BigDeal was excited to be getting out of jail, but he had no clue who posted his bail. LilGuy was dead, Dowe was dead, and his family didn't really fuck with him like that. Nonetheless, his bail was paid and he wasn't about to sit around and wait for them to say it was a mistake.

While packing his things all BigDeal could do was think about getting at Jünior and Phenöm. The little niggas that he thought were easy licks turned out to be just a tad bit more thorough than he gave credit for.

"Yo, let me get yo pillow too." Jetter said, as he stuffed the food that BigDeal gave him into his bin.

"Nigga, I don't give a fuck about that shit!" BigDeal shot back, standing near the door with his paperwork and the little bit of clothes that he had acquired since being there in his hands.

Jetter walked over and peaced BigDeal, before saying, "Be easy, big bruh."

"No doubt, and you keep ya head up in here. Niggas goin try you now that I'm gone, hold that shit up, ya'heard?"

"Butler, let's go, nigga!" Ofc. Browards yelled, starting to get aggravated.

"I'm coming, motherfucka!"

"Hurry up and get outta here, nigga." an inmate yelled through the doors.

"Nigga act like he don't wanna leave and shit." another inmate joined in, standing at his cell door envious that he wasn't the one going home.

"If you don't wanna go, I'll take yo place!" the kid next to BigDeal's cell offered, as BigDeal slid his cell door shut.

"Yeah aight, nigga, keep dreaming on that shit." BigDeal laughed, walking towards the front of the unit.

"You got everything?" Ofc. Browards asked, looking BigDeal up and down with disgust.

"Yeah, now pop these doors." he returned with excitement spilling over, now ready to go.

"Don't worry, you'll be back by the end of the month!" Ofc. Browards shot back, hitting the button to let BigDeal off the unit.

"Yeah aight, don't hold your motherfucking breath on that shit." BigDeal returned, walking off the unit with his chest poked out.

Being released from jail was the greatest feeling ever. BigDeal was anxious to get home so that he could grab his gun, get something to eat, and fuck his girlfriend, just in that order. He made it to reception where he was handed the clothes that he was arrested in.

Once BigDeal was dressed he sat in front for about 45 minutes before his paperwork was ready. They had to make sure that he didn't have any outstanding warrants anywhere else before releasing him. During this process most guys thought that they were going to be returned to their unit, stating that they couldn't leave. Nonetheless, when the papers were put in his hands to sign, BigDeal quickly signed, and hauled ass out of there.

Walking down the ramp in the front of the green monster, BigDeal saw the #25 bus sitting at the bus stop. He put a little bit more pep in his step, even more anxious than before.

"Yo, you got change for $5.00, my nigga?" a dude asked, walking up behind BigDeal.

"Motherfucka, do it look like I got change!?" he shot back, turning around to see who he was talking to.

"I'm saying ---"

"Yo, nigga!" Phenöm called out, hopping from behind a car just feet away with a AK-47 in his hands. "This 'fore shooting my homegirl!"

"Fuck!" BigDeal gasped, seeing the smile on Ghoon's face as he now stood in front of BigDeal with his .380 aimed at BigDeal's midsection.

"Ain't this about a bitch!" he thought to himself, realizing just who had bailed him out now.

TAT, TAT, BOK, TAT, BOK, BOK, TAT, BOK, TAT, TAT, TAT, TAT, TAT, TAT, TAT !!!!!

"Come on, nigga, let's go!" Phenöm ordered, taking off to the car that Doug had just pulled up in front of them in.

"Faggot ass nigga!" Ghoon barked at a now dead BigDeal, as he made his way to the car.

"That's for Sofi, nigga!" Doug said, as Ghoon and Phenöm hopped in the car.

SCCUUURRRRR !!!

Tuesday April 11th, 2018

6:18 p.m.
Osborne Terrace
■ Newark ■

"Where the fuck is my money, nigga?" Sul questioned, as Boyn and Laavell helped the young hustler upside down from the building on the corner of Tillinghast Street.

"Man, I told you already, I was gonna pay you this Friday, my girl gets paid then."

"Did he give your girl the shit or did you openly take this man's shit and dip off with his money?" Boyn questioned, ready to release the kid's leg.

"Sul, I swear on my kid's lives, I'll have your money come Friday, please!"

"So you think that my time is dictated by when you're ready to pay me, huh?"

"Nah, I just figured that you would unders ---"

"Drop is ass!" Sul ordered, turning around to walk away.

"Please, don't, I swear ---" the kid pleaded, before Boyn and Laavell let his legs go. "Aaaahhhhhhh!!!"

"Now that's how you take the trash out!" Boyn laughed, walking away from the ledge.

The kid's body fell 4 stories hitting the railing at the bottom that led to the basement, his neck snapping instantly, blood splashing in every direction. Sul walked away lighting his cigar without a second thought as to what had just taken place, he was getting used to this shit all over again. Rasul *Sul*

Melvin was the man in charge of an elite drug empire and though he was in charge on the streets, he was still second in command behind Fahim. Fahim was running his empire from prison on the low through Sul since his being sentenced to life in prison.

Sul was Fahim's #2 guy in Newark as well as his lifeline to the outside world. Because Sul made sure that Fahim's operation was still running, Fahim had Sul living wonderfully at the age of 41, and Sul couldn't complain. Fahim was a part of something that he just couldn't walk away from even if he wanted to. There were plenty of times when he wanted to reach out and take care of his family, but the brothers made it clear that death was the key to breaking their oath. There was now a table built amongst three men that met in dangerous circumstances. Aiyùk and his twin brother Aiyòk both sat at the table along with their older brother Aiyàk. Fahim landed a position with Aiyàk that

Sul was born in Newark and grew up on 19th Street and 19th Avenue but couldn't stay out of prison, Sul was just finishing up a 15 year prison bid a little over a year ago. While Sul was locked up his little brother Tarin had been running with a few people that put him in position to pass something down to his big brother, Tarin was serving 500 months in the feds. Sul couldn't thank Tarin enough for plugging him in with Fahim because he needed that, Sul came home to more money than he had ever seen in his life and he was worth a smooth $2,000,000.00. Sul was running multiple businesses for Fahim and moving even more drugs than Fahim was moving when he was home. Fahim was a part of the East Coast Crime Syndicate and there wasn't anything that he could do to get out other than stuffing a pine box with his body. Sul wasn't a part of that society even though he wanted to be, he was just the front man on the streets for Fahim because he couldn't be there.

A small crowd began to form as Sul stepped out of the building nonchalantly, headed towards his white Lincoln Navigator. Boyn and Laavell came out of the building laughing and conversing, keeping their guilty expressions hidden from the world. Sul climbed into the SUV and continued watching *In Living Color*. Sul had *In Living Color* playing on the 7" screen that was hanging from the ceiling of the SUV. This was a show that Sul watched every chance that he got. Boyn walked around the SUV and climbed in the backseat next to Sul. Laavell climbed into the passenger seat, still laughing at the way the kid screamed on his way down.

"Larry, get us away from this motherfucka." Laavell said, lighting up his Black-n-Mild.

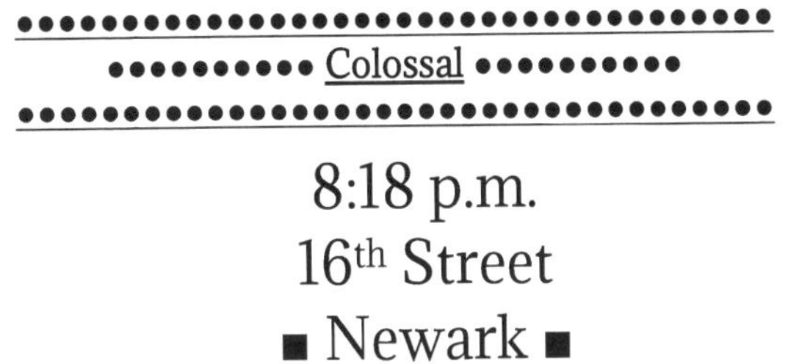

"How many niggas did Jünior say was up in there?" Phenöm asked, sitting in the backseat of the royal blue rental Buick Regal LS.

"It's three niggas in there other than Troy, she's not on the clock but she's do ---"

"Man, I don't care about all of that!" Phenöm snapped, cutting Chämp off as he shoved bullet after bullet into the magazine of his new .45 desert eagle with the extended clip.

"Relax, Johnnie, it's not that serious." Doug jumped in, sitting there holding her chrome glock .380.

Doug knew that Chämp and Phenöm had been beefing about how they had rushed into Cynt's apartment yesterday, Cynt had been cursing him out about it. Cynt didn't find anything remotely funny about Phenöm's situation, and figured none of his friends should be finding time to clown around about it. Phenöm and Cynt argued about the situation for a few minutes and then they had wild make-up sex, after that Phenöm had time to think about it and realized that Cynt was right. When he said something to Chämp about it Chämp tried to make fun of Cynt, and that's when Phenöm and Chämp got into it.

"He good, trust me and you, Johnnie don't wanna go there with me again." Chämp shot back, looking in the rearview mirror at Phenöm.

"Hhmmph!" Phenöm huffed, choosing to leave the situation alone for right now.

The last time that Phenöm had tried to disrespect Chämp punkingly, Chämp had called Phenöm out for a fair one in Jünior's backyard. Of course Phenöm didn't turn down the fade and they ended up fighting, Chämp got the best of Phenöm that day and now felt like he could take Phenöm at any given time. Chämp was very calm, cool, and collective but he was far from a push over, Chämp could throw down when it came to the hands. Phenöm was serious with the hands as well but that day Chämp had gotten the best of him, however, over the years Phenöm was up on Chämp when it came to their fights. Phenöm was up one on Chämp and Chämp was one up on Jünior, it was something that they did more often when they were younger but since they were growing they fought less.

Phenöm was pissed off that Jünior had even sent Chämp on this lick [robbery] instead of Tàbi as planned, Phenöm didn't feel as though Chämp was built for this type of thing. This was a lick that Jünior and Troy had been planning for awhile now, and with Troy's help he finally had everything that he needed to make it happen. This was a low key work and stash house for a big time pusher, Jünior didn't know who the spot belonged to but in the end he really didn't care!

After everything that Troy had told Jünior he had estimated there to be about $200,000.00 worth of money and drugs within the spot, a lick well worth hitting. Jünior didn't want to really get mixed back up in the life after what happened to his father, so he would send Phenöm and Troy on licks that would help put money in their pockets. Jünior knew right of the top that he wasn't about to go on a long binge with whatever drugs that he came off with, he was going to move the work and that was it. He knew all too well what the life could do to you so he was hitting this thing with a blueprinted plan, he was about to set the tone for his future. Jünior had Nya looking into all types of investments that he was going to jump into, he wasn't about to pick up where his father left off.

'We still hustle till the sun come up/ crack a forty when the sun go down/ it's a cold winter/ y'all niggas better bundle up/ and I bet it be a hotter summer/ grab a onion just to lock it down/ you hot now, listen up..........'

"Yo, turn that shit the fuck down!" Phenöm barked, after Chämp turned Freeway's *What We Do* featuring Jay Z and Beanie Sigel up higher than it needed to be.

"Word, you wild'n right now, bruh!" Doug jumped in, shooting Chämp the coldest stare.

"My bad, this my shit, I forgot where I was at for a second."

"This why I fucking told this nigga that this was a bad idea." Phenöm said, shaking his head with disappointment.

"Well, we here now and we gotta work with what we working with." Doug told him.

"Look, we goin' run up in there, dead everything, and be ---"

"Hold up, when you say dead everything you talking about killing everybody up in there?" Chämp asked, with shock written all over his face, looking towards Doug for confirmation.

"Congratulations, somebody get this motherfucka a Scooby snack for catching on so gotdamn easily!" Phenöm clowned, as two teenage girls walked pass the Regal LS. "Doug, as soon as we get in between the houses, pull this bitch around the corner. This ain't goin' take but 5 minutes tops, and we'll be coming out."

"Aight, say less." she replied, looking in her mirror as a red Family cab rode by headed toward Avon Avenue.

"This is some bullshit!"

"Nigga, shut up and bring your ass on!" Phenöm ordered, opening his door and climbing out.

Phenöm quickly jogged in between the two houses that sat in the middle of the block, carrying his .38 and his .45 down at his side. He was draped in his black Carhartt one-piece overall jumper, with a pair of black leather Timberlands, he was ready to get down and handle his business at all time. Chämp hopped out of thee Regal LS looking back at Doug trying to see if she was give him any indication that what Phenöm was saying was a go, he didn't want any parts of anybody's murder. He looked from his left to his right nervously before following behind Phenöm, silently cursing Jünior out for sending him on this wild goose chase with Phenöm.

Chämp was wearing a pair of blue Rocawear jeans, black G-Unit low top sneakers, and a black fitted, he refused to wear his good clothes for this. They both pressed their back against the outside of the house and waited for Doug to pull off before proceeding, everything had to go as planned. Jünior had timed everything down to a "T" so Phenöm knew he couldn't waste a blink of a second, his reason why he wished that Jünior wouldn't have sent Chämp.

There was another group of guys in the house across the street from the workhouse, this was the house that the workers sat in when not on the clock. Whoever was running this work house had his workers pulling 72 hour shifts at a time, so when they weren't bagging up or counting money, they were across the street waiting their turn. Jünior knew the times that the bulk of them went across the street for their ten minute break, so Phenöm and Chämp had less than ten minutes to get in and out.

This was Chämp's first time really deep in the mix of things, and needless to say he was so nervous that he was shitting bricks! First off, he didn't have a gun, so he had to depend on Phenöm throughout this whole ordeal, and that didn't sit too well with him. Then Chämp really didn't like their odds against all of the dudes that Troy had told them were surrounding the house, he knew that Phenöm was a sharp shooter as was Bruce Willis on the movie *The Last Man Standing.*

Both Chämp and Phenöm ran to the back of the yard and hopped the back fence. The back fence was the only thing separating 15th Street from 16th Street. They scanned the whole backyard before making a move towards the house 16th Street. The duo knew that somebody could've been back there. Phenöm led the way with both of his guns aimed high. Oh how he was ready to put a bullet in any and everything that stood in their way.

Chämp's heart was racing a mile a minute as they neared the back door. They pressed their bodies against the house and Chämp took a deep breath. Chämp looked up to the bathroom window which Doug had left unlocked before they got there. She had left a ladder right underneath the window for them to climb up on. These were the exact plans that Jünior had mapped out for them. Doug just happened to follow every detail down to the very last scribble.

Phenöm started up the ladder first, skipping every other step as he was so anxious to get up in the apartment. Phenöm literally lived for this type of shit! Chämp was hot on Phenöm's trail, promising himself that if he made it out of this alive, he was never again doing no shit like this!

As Phenöm neared the window he'd heard one of the dudes walk into the bathroom and close the door. Chämp ran right into Phenöm because he had to stop right where he was at. Phenöm was right at the tip of the window seal peeking into the bathroom, looking right at the dude's back.

The dude stood there releasing his bladder which was full of Coronas.

Phenöm wanted to shoot the kid in the back of his head right then and there. However, Phenöm knew that that wasn't a part of the plan at that moment, so he had to wait. To an excited and anxious Phenöm it felt like the kid was pissing from hours. It took him 2 minutes to piss, it was like this nigga had the bladder of a racehorse! Without washing his hands the kid walked back into the living room, leaving the door halfway open instead of closing it back the way it was.

Phenöm and Chämp crept into the bathroom having to be extremely careful. They crept towards the door to see how the dudes were positioned within the living room. Everybody were sitting in the living room with their backs towards the bathroom. They were watching the fiendishly amazing Paradice Charms getting fucked on the porno, *Let Off In Me*. Doug was the only female in the room and she was sitting front and center.

She stood there with nothing but her thong and bra on looking like something to eat! She had held the dudes off for as long as she could, but the movie was painting all kinds of pictures for them. Lined up against the wall near the front door was 4 nice size totes right where Doug said they'd be, she had come through for Jünior once again. It was definitely hard to keep these dudes off of her because they'd been trying to get with her since she started working there six months ago, because Doug was bad!

"Come here, Cassey, help me massage this tension between my legs." the dude that had just left the bathroom said, as Phenöm slowly moved towards them.

"Nah, I want her to tell me how many licks it's goin take to get to the center of this tootsie roll pop!" the dude to Doug's left said, openly stroking his dick for all to see.

"Why don't I masturbate this desert eagle to the sweet sound of y'all screaming for mercy!?" Phenöm jumped in, obviously disgusted at how they spoke to Doug.

"Huh!" one dude gasped, quickly turning around to see Phenöm and Chämp standing there.

"What the fuck!" the kid with his dick in his hand replied.

"Nigga, do you know who shit you're fucking wi ---" the last kid began, before Phenöm found salvation within both of his trigger fingers.

BOK, BOK, POP, BOK, POP, BOK.....POP, POP..........BOK !!!

"About fucking time!" Doug spat, as she quickly grabbed her clothes and started putting on her blue True Religion jeans, not at all fazed by the scene before her. "Another minute and I was undoubtedly about to be raped in this bitch!"

"I don't know, you might've actually like it." Phenöm returned, standing there in the thick of gun smoke and debris lusting over Doug's body, holding his guns at his side.

"Damn!" Chämp mumbled, seeing Doug's curves for the first time and finding himself getting an erection.

"Fuck you, Phenöm."

"Ummm, can....we get.....the fuck outta here?" Chämp asked, trying to keep his eyes off of Doug, and keep from throwing up at the same time.

Pulling her blue True Religion shirt over her head as quickly as she could, Doug said, "Yes, lets."

While Doug was getting dressed, Phenöm ran into the back room and went straight for the closet. There he found a bookbag filled with drugs and another bookbag filled with cash. He opened them up to check the contents. Seeing what they came for, Phenöm zipped both bags back up and left the room. When he stepped into the living room he saw Chämp handing Doug another bookbag. His eyes lit up when he saw yet another bookbag, thinking that it had more drugs in it.

"Come on, let's get the fuck outta here." Chämp hissed, as he started to get a funny feeling in his stomach.

"I could not agree with you more." Doug joined in, tossing the bookbag onto her back as she made her way towards the back door.

Phenöm pulled his phone out and called Troy to tell her that they were coming out. Troy answered the phone on the first ring, "Yo?"

"We coming out, pull up." Phenöm returned, walking out of the door leaving it wide open.

"That shit was crazy." Doug said, walking down the back hallway steps that lead to the slide of the house. "I honestly didn't think we was goin' get away with that shit. My gut was feeling uneasy the whole time."

"Shit, I knew we was goin' get that off as soon as y'all put me on." Phenöm replied, just a step ahead of her with a blue and black bookbag on his back. Still in his right hand was his Desert Eagle.

"And how the fuck you know that, genius?" Chämp questioned, his heart still racing with nervousness, as he followed behind Doug who was also carrying a bookbag on her back.

"Fuck you mean? The moment that y'all told me, I knew a real nigga was goin' be in the vicinity! That's how, motherfucka." Phenöm shot back, as the 3 of them reached the driveway of the house and spotted Troy parked at the end of the driveway in a rented Buick Regal LS.

"This nigga!" Chämp said under his breath, as they walked out into the front yard.

"Y'all niggas hurry up 'fore we ---" Troy began, before they all heard shots ringing out from across the street.

"Shit!" Chämp gasped, as his body went into a complete circle before he hit the ground. A bullet ripped into Chämps left arm, causing him to say, "Fuck!"

"Get in the fucking car now!" Phenöm barked at Doug, firing his .45 back while going to check on Chämp. "You good?"

"I'm hit, nigga!"

"Come on, y'all!" Troy yelled, as bullets tore into the Regal causing Doug and Troy to duck down.

"Open the door!" Phenöm shot back, shooting Kart while trying to help Chämp to his feet.

"Nah, nigga, y'all ain't going nowhere!" Unfi yelled, as Phenöm shot Tuppa that was behind Unfi.

"Hurry up!" Doug shrieked, as Chämp jumped into the passenger seat.

Phenöm stood beside the Regal aiming over the roof of the car, letting off three more shots, before telling Troy, "Go head, let's get outta here!"

Troy sped off across 16th Street headed towards Madison Avenue as Unfi stood in the middle of the street. Tuppa stood up clutching his left shoulder as Kart still lie on the ground holding his stomach.

9:22 p.m.
Bergen Street
▪ Newark ▪

"Erik, where are you at, you know we were supposed to be at my mother's house an hour ago." Mrs. Perkins informed through the phone, as she sat home in their living room dress for dinner at her mother's.

"You go ahead, I was just called to a case on the way home." Ofc. Perkins replied, racing his red 2008 Ram 1500 Rebel across Bergen Street headed towards Avon Avenue.

"Oh, boy, why can't Dwayne take this one and fill you in about the details later?"

"Dwayne's at another crime scene over on 9th Ave., he's the reason that they called me to this one."

"I swear, this shit is getting so fucking old, I might as well be fucking single!" she spat, as Ofc. Perkins drove through Avon Avenue's intersection.

"Don't say that, you make me feel for doing my job."

"Good, cause you also have a job at home taking care of your fucking wife, that you are doing horrible at might I add!"

"Teresa, I told you that I was going to be spending more time at home once I get this promotion." he replied, preparing to make a right turn up Madison Avenue.

"Whatever, Erik, I'm just about to get me a boyfriend on the side or something!"

"Baby, don't talk like that, I promise that I'm going to turn my phone off all day tomorrow, so that it's just you and me, okay?" Ofc. Perkins said, not even realizing that his wife had already hung up after her statement. "Hello…hello, Teresa?"

Ofc. Perkins look at his phone and saw that the call had been over, so he sat his phone on the passenger seat as he neared 11th Street. He knew that he was neglecting his wife in the worse way, but he was just trying to get his promotion that he was up for so that he could do more for and with her. But his wife couldn't understand that in order for him to get the promotion he had to put in the time, and solve some of the hard cases that were still open. As he turned onto 11th Street he noticed three figures in dark colored suits, climbing into a black 2013 Volvo S60 with limousine dark tinted windows.

The Volvo S60 pulled off riding right pass Ofc. Perkins's 1500 Rebel, as he was parking behind the crowd of people that were standing around. Ofc. Perkins climbed out of the 1500 Rebel and walked over to the crowd looking pass tem at the many shell casings, he was definitely at the right place. While looking for dead bodies he couldn't get the three suits out of his head, and then the fact that there were so many shell casings and no bodies. Ofc. Perkins walked up to a uniformed Ofc. and flashed his badge, he let him know that he was the leading Dt. on the case.

"What's going on, Dt.?"

"Another day on the job, what do we have?" Ofc. Perkins replied, pulling out a pack of Newport shorts.

"Two dead inside and one on his way to U.M.D. in critical condition."

"And who were the three spooks that just took off?"

"F.B.I., of course."

Ofc. Perkins held his lighter in mid-air with the flame dancing just in front of his cigarette, as he replied, "The feds?"

11:04 p.m.
S. 14th Street
▪ Newark ▪

"Aaaggghhh! Please, I swear it wasn't ---"

"Shut the fuck up, when Sul's money comes up short then my motherfucking money come up short! And I don't have the sympathy for the nigga that caused that!" Boyn barked standing over Pree who was tied to the chair drenched in blood.

"I swear to God, Boyn, it wasn't me, man!"

"Who was left in charge of your block? You! Who hands did I put the drugs in? Yours! So who do I blame? YOU!" he snapped, swinging the hammer with deadly force, crashing into Pree's collar bone.

"Aaaggghhhhhh!"

"Pain is the answer for your fuck up, but death will compensate for the loss that I just took."

Boyn stood in the center of an abandoned basement with a construction worker's tool belt wrapped around his waist, delivering pain to his cousin and one of the soldiers that he'd hand picked to run one of his blocks. Behind him were 3 beefed up body guards staring on as Boyn inflicted sheer pain upon Pree. Behind them was the head nigga in charge, Sul, sitting in a black lawn chair smoking a $1,200.00 Gurkha Black Dragon cigar, overseeing the work of his top soldier. The room was dim but lit by the street lights outside, crashing against each wall, just lighting the room enough to leave the wondrous rats in fear.

The room smelled of cigar smoke, old piss, mold, dog shit, and stale living, however, Boyn was used to the stench because of repeated trips down there. Pree was tied down to a wooden chair by rusted chains, with his 2 top soldiers beside him, their clothes had been stripped from their bodies other than their boxers. The other 2 kids had their mouths duct taped shut, with their eyes wandering around the room for any sign of hope. Boyn gave Pree one more reassuring smile before drawing his chrome P-89 ruger, aiming it at Pree's head, and wrapped his finger around the trigger.

"Please, Sul, I'm begging you not to do this." Pree pleaded, pissing flowing down his leg from excruciating fear. "I can make this right, I swear on my life!"

"Now you see, that's where we have a problem because your life means nothing to me any more." he countered, his face straightening back up.

"Please!!!"

"Shut the fuck up!"

BLOK, BLOK, BLOK, BLOK, BLOK !!!

Pree's body jerked forcefully as each bullet entered his body effortlessly, blood splattered in several different directions, painting Boyn's grey True Religion T-shirt, the walls, and the floor. You could hear the pounding of the other 2 soldier's heart as they witnessed their close friend murdered, a fate that they dreaded meeting. Boyn walked over towards the kid to his left and raised the gun carelessly. The young boy began to tussle violently trying to fight for his freedom. Boyn put a bullet in his head without a blink of the eye, the boy's head snapped back as his blood created a pattern against the wall behind him. Next he walked over to the third hustler and pressed the smoking hot barrel against his forehead, causing the kid to squirm from the pain.

"You're gonna make sure that this never happens again, you go back out there and regroup. You find out who caused my money to come up short, and trust that if this happens again I'm gonna kill you and your entire family." Boyn admitted, staring the kid square in his eyes. "Make sure that you never forget this night."

The kid nodded his head as Boyn turned around and looked at Sul, Sul nodded his head, before saying, "Clean this up and get back to work, I gotta go outta town for a while and when I get back I expect things to be back to business as usual."

"I got this." he said, watching Sul stand up with the calm of no return as his phone began to vibrate. "Y'all heard what he said, get this shit cleaned up and make sure this motherfucka gets back to the block in one piece."

"Speak." Sul said into his phone, walking out of the room. You could tell that he he had just received some fucked up news because he stopped instantly, and yell, "Are you fucking kidding me right now! You motherfuckas are the dumbest son-of-a-bitches I've ever known!"

"Sul, what's the word?" Boyn asked, once Sul threw his phone against the wall shattering it into pieces.

"My main motherfucking spot just got hit!"

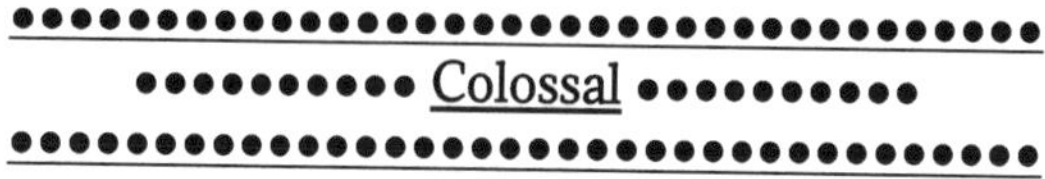

11:53 p.m.
Farley Avenue
■ Newark ■

"Daddy, can you start the game for us?" Monique asked, walking into Jünior's room with Ciara in tow, both with ketchup and mustard on their faces.

"Yeah, give me a se ---" Jünior began, as he lifted his head to look at his daughter's direction, seeing them both standing there looking cute as ever in his T-shirts, hair all wild, tongues out in the corners of their mouths trying to lick off the ketchup and mustard. Jünior burst into laughter before saying, "Both of y'all come here."

"What matter, daddy, why come you laughed with us?" Ciara asked, as they approached him.

"Not why come, it's how come." he corrected, laughing even harder as both girls walked into his outstretched arms, wrapping their little arms around his neck returning his hug. Jünior gently kissed both of them on their messy cheeks before saying, "And I'm laughing because you two are just too damn cute, and I love y'all."

"We love you, too." Monique replied lovingly.

"Now can you start us game for bed?" Ciara asked, quickly kissing her father on his right cheek, a trick that her and Monique picked up to ensure that they get their way. It was a trick that Jünior knew all too well but each time that they did it to him it still melted his heart turning him into putty in their hands.

"Yes, I'll start the game for y'all right after y'all go tell gandma to wipe your faces off."

"Okay!" the girls excitedly exclaimed in cheerful unison, before taking off out of the room to find Jackie.

Jünior shook his head while still he enjoyed the warm smile that spread across his face, it was nothing like spending time with his girls. Being on house arrest was nothing to Jünior because he was home with his kids, still dealing with Sofi being in a coma and BigDeal still breathing, that was killing him. Then he had the issue of finding the right lawyer for Phenöm, at times Jünior felt the walls were closing in on him when he looked at what was on his shoulders. The only thing that made any sense these days to Jünior was Ciara, Monique, Mir, Nya, and Nique, they were his main focus as of late. Speaking of Nique, she was on a mission to get pregnant lately, Jünior couldn't understand for the life of him why she wanted a baby so bad by him. They both were very young with two kids and no jobs, Nique did have her own apartment but it was still a struggle.

Jünior was sitting there reading a book titled, Bad Apple - The Baddest Chick [part 1], written by the beautiful Nisa Santiago, the first of an exciting page dropping trilogy. Jünior stood up and sat the book on top of the stack of books that Nya had bought him, he had asked her to pick him up a bunch of them. While locked up Jünior had read a few books such as, Cartier Cartel by Nisa Santiago, Cruel Execution - Come In Peace Or Leave In Pieces by Duquie Wilson, Bad blood part 1 and 2 by the brother Tuffy, Animal parts 1,2,3, and 4 by K'wan, Thugs Cry by Cash, and The Last Of A

Dying Breed by Akbar Prey. Jünior had read each of those books while he was in the Green Monster, and promised himself that he would read a book a day when got home. He walked over to his 32 inch flat screen and turned his Playstation 2 on for the girls, setting up Tetris so that they could just grab the controllers and play when they came back. He sat back down and started thinking about the lick that Phenöm and Chämp had pulled the other day, Phenöm had called and let him know that everything was a go but Jünior was waiting on Chämp to bring him the money.

Nique and Nya had been out having a drink at Applebee's on Bergen Street and Springfield Avenue, ever since Jünior had been home Nique had been leaving the girls with their father and hitting the town with Nya, since Jünior couldn't move in with her yet, Nique and Monique was staying at Jackie's house at least five days out of the week. Ever since Phenöm and Chämp hit that lick the other night on 11th Street, they had been laying low because of the third victim that was still fighting for his life. Jünior told them to lie as low as they could until he found what was what from Koji, so far everything was clear but Jünior just wanted to make sure.

Nya and Nique pulled up in front of Jackie's house both a little tipsy, Nique gave Nya a hug and then climbed out of the Lacrosse. She rang the doorbell and Mir came downstairs to let her in, she couldn't just walk in because she didn't have a key. Nique walked into the house with her shopping bags and left overs from Applebee's, Mir was right behind her closing the door as Nique proceeded towards Jünior's bedroom.

"Girl, Gina said that her landlord is tripping talking about putting her out because of it." Nique told Tàbi, as she walked into the bedroom with her baby blue Galaxy S3 to her right ear.

"That's so fucked up, I can't believe what Gina is going through." Tàbi replied, knowing that she was the one that gave Ofc. Perkins's source the false information that sent the police to Gina's house.

"I know, right." Nique expressed, leaning in and kissing Jünior on his lips as he sat on the bed while Monique and Ciara were playing Tetris. "Hey, bae, what you reading?"

"The Baddest Chick part 1." he answered.

"Mommy!" the girls cheered, jumping up to hug Nique as she sat on the bed to Jünior's right.

"I take it you're in the house, now." Tàbi pointed out, just as Nique had removed her phone from her ear to hug her and kiss her babies.

"Hey, my babies!" Nique exclaimed overly excited, with her arms open for the girls to collapse into her embrace, after sitting her S3 on the bed. "I missed y'all so much while I was out with auntie Shenya and auntie Cynt! Was y'all good for daddy and gandma Jackie while mommy was gone?"

"Daddy prayed kitchen wit us and dress up." Ciara excitedly confessed, climbing up onto Nique's lap opposite Monique who had already claimed Nique' right leg.

"Oh, he did, did he?"

"Uh-huh. And, and, and he played color books with us, too." Monique replied, as Nique leaned over and gave Jünior another kiss on his lips.

"Wow," Nique gasped, smiling endlessly because her girls had a great father in their lives. "You guys are lucky to have a dad that does great things with you, right?"

"Yeah!" both girls cheered in unison.

"Not lucky, but blessed." Jünior said, as his 2S began to vibrate. "We're Muslim, we don't believe in luck, we are blessed through the mercy and grace of, Allah."

"Who is that?" Nique questioned, as Jünior looked at his phone to see who was texting him.

"None ya!"

"Don't play with me Mustafa."

■ **Doug** ■
The food is ready, you
want me to bring it to you now?

"I'm not playing, it's none ya texting me." he laughed, texting Doug back.

"Excuse me, girls, mommy needs to get hands on with daddy real quick cause he thinks that I'm playing with him" Nique said, letting the girls down off of her lap. "Jünior, who the fuck are you texting?"

"Oooh, mommy cursing!" the girls teased, pointing their little index fingers at Nique.

"I know," Jünior replied, turning to face a upset Nique, "And she better watch her mouth in front of y'all."

"I'm sorry, girls, y'all go ahead and tell grandma to run y'all a bath so I can put y'all to bed." Nique returned, focusing back on Jünior. "Mustafa Raheem, who are you texting?"

"None ya damn business!" he replied jokingly, as the girls stood there smiling, while he was pressing the send button just before Nique aggressively snatched the phone out of his hands.

■ **Jünior** ■
Nah, bring it to me in the
morning, my baby cooked already

"Oooohh, you lucky," Nique snapped, after finding out that Jünior was texting Chämp and not some chick. "Stop playing with me, Mustafa, I will hurt a bitch over mine!"

"Awwww, you look so cute when you get jealous." he said, grabbing her chin and lightly squeezing it, as Nique sat his phone on the bed between them.

"Don't touch me, you play too damn much!" she said, swatting his hand away from her chin.

"You sure you don't me touching you?" Jünior asked, wrapping his arms around her and pulling her into a bear hug.

"Stop, get off of me." Nique smiled, pulling away from Jünior, standing up and running towards the door, while saying, "Come on girls, it's time to take y'all bath so y'all can get ready for bed."

"Do we have to?" Monique whined, running over to her father and wrapping her arms around his right leg.

"Yes you have to now let's go, both of y'all." she said, as Ciara followed her sister and grabbed Jünior's left leg, both giving him the puppy dog eyes.

"Daddy, we not tired." Monique whined.

"I said lets go, mommy and daddy wanna spend some alone time together."

"Y'all go ahead and take y'all baths and then go lay with grandma and watch t.v. until you fall asleep." Jünior told them, knowing that they weren't going to budge if he didn't say something.

"So we not have to go bed?" Ciara asked, laying her little head on Jünior's knee.

"Yes, y'all are going to be ---"

"No, y'all can go in the room with grandma and watch TV, but if y'all don't be good then I'm putting y'all to bed."

"We goin' be good." the girls yelled excitedly, running out of the room.

"I can't stand yo ass!" Nique said, looking at him with squinted eyes, feeling like his was taking control of her girls. "You got that for now, but wait until mommy gets her power back."

"Whatever, go bathe the kids and bring your ass back so that I can do some things to that pussy!" he replied.

"Just nasty." Nique smiled blushingly.

Nique pulled her earrings out of her ears and laid them atop of Jünior's nightstand, then slid out of her light blue Seven jeans. She didn't have far to walk to put her clothes in the dirty clothes hamper because the closet was right there just feet away from the bed, the room had become even more over crowded now that Nique and Monique was there.

Jünior picked his book back up and began reading again as Nique walked the girls out of the room in her white g-string and T-shirt, causing Jünior to watch as her ass cheeks bounced sexily with each step. Jünior's dick instantly became erect just from looking at Nique's ass, he couldn't deny that he had a beautiful woman and even though he lusted over other women, he had the total package with Dominique Perez!

Tuesday April 13th, 2018

2:13 p.m.
Chadwick Avenue
▪ Newark ▪

"Did you talk to Chämp yet?" Doug asked Troy, as they sat in Nya's Lacrosse which was parked on the corner of Chadwick Avenue right behind building 100.

"Nah, he hasn't answered any of my calls since we dumped his ass at the hospital the other night." Troy replied, bobbing her head to Nas' One Mic as it leaked out of the speakers.

"Well, is the nigga alive at least?"

"Yeah, Jünior said that he text him the next day, you know how these niggas be in their feelings and shit worse than bitches!"

"Hell yeah."

"Doug, pass me those two ditches from between the seat." Tàbi yelled from the gate, where she was sitting in her beach chair.

"Damn, didn't y'all hoes just smoke a blunt!" Rae asked, while serving a fiend three bags of dope.

"I'm telling you." Paul joined in, snaking his neck sassily.

"Didn't you just drink a Bud Ice?" Nique asked, passing Tàbi a bag of sour diesel [weed].

"Bitch, don't worry about how many beers that I drink, I don't drink nearly as much as y'all smoke." Rae snapped, taking a gulp of her 24oz can of Bud Ice.

"Here, Tab." Doug called out, holding the two vanilla dutch masters out of the window in her right hand.

"Where the fuck is Nya?" Troy questioned, looking towards the building.

"Ladies, ladies." 7re greeted, walking up on them with two of his little homies in tow.

"7re, what's good?" Tàbi returned, while grabbing the cigars from Doug.

"I can't call it, Nique, let me holla at you real quick."

"What's up?" Nique asked, standing up and walking towards him.

"Here, this is another six stacks [thousand] to go towards the homegirl's medical bills," 7re answered, handing Nique the money while looking her up and down. "Still no word on the nigga BigDeal?"

"Jünior said that he got it handled and y'all can chill out, he said that BigDeal goin' be meeting his brothers real soon." she replied, smiling at that fact that her man was handling business as he promised.

"Aight, tell son that I appreciate everything that he's done for Sofi, that's real nigga shit, and if he needs anything to just let me know."

"I sure will."

"How's Sofi holding up?"

"7re, stop staring at me like that, nigga, you like my big brother!" Nique spat, feeling uncomfortable with the way he was staring at her titties.

"My bad, you getting thick, girl, you better tell Jünior to keep a leash on you, niggas be checking for you."

"Whatever, the only nigga that can touch this is Mustafa Raheem, know that!" Nique spat, letting it be known who she belonged to.

"Lucky him!" 7re returned, licking his lips seductively.

"Whatever, we just came from seeing Sofi, she's still the same so I guess that's a good thing, seeing how she hasn't gotten worse." she informed him, while stuffing the money into her green Michael Kors handbag.

"Trillz, that's what's up, look, you go ahead and put that money up before something happens to it." 7re said, as a cherry top police car drove up Madison Avenue.

"Yeah, you right."

"Later, beautiful."

"Aight, 7re." Nique said, as they embraced in a hug, just as Nya wa coming out of the building carrying a black Nike book bag.

Two fiends walked up to the building with a Pathmark shopping cart full of crushed cans and steel pipes, they walked right up to Paul and Rae. Paul stood near the back door of building 100 in a pair of skin tight white JCME jeggings, a pink True Religion T-shirt, and a pair of pink Nike ACG boots. Though Paul was a homosexual and was blatantly flamboyant with his sexual preference, he knew that he was a man and not a women. Paul would ride for his homegirls in the blink of an eye, he just happens to be more attracted to men instead of women. Jünior, Chämp, and Phenöm never judged Paul because they knew what Paul was into, before he was fully confident enough to admit it to himself.

Jünior had fought many dudes that tried to clown or attack Paul because of who he was, Paul didn't have Aids nor was he contagious. No, Jünior wasn't into the whole homosexual thing, however, him and Paul grew up together since they were little kids and he loved him like a brother. The crew let it be known that Paul was one of them and if you fucked with him, you had to fuck with Jünior, Phenöm, and the entire the family. Paul and Rae were the ones that put the most work in on the block, they really did the hand to hand while Doug and Tàbi collected the money. Troy and Nique usually did the packaging since Mona, Lissa, and Chelia were locked up, and Nya did the negotiating for them.

7re broke their embrace and turned to leave as he savored the lingering scent of Nique's Paris Hilton CanCan perfume, heading back towards Clinton Avenue. 7re knew that Nique was a rare breed and he had tried to make several moves on her, but Nique was dead lock faithful to her man. Every time that 7re or any other dude made an advance at her, Nique would let Jünior know immediately which caused him to respect and love her that much more.

As 7re walked off his little homies all took in Nique's appearance as she stood there in her brown Hermes halter mini dress with the exposingly enticing neckline, showing off her succulent cleavage. On her feet were a pair of green and brown Hermes soft bottom sneakers, this was a outfit that cost her all of the money that she had saved up. Nique's hair was done up in blonde Marley twist which were dark brown at the root, pulled into a ponytail so that she could show off her new tattoo.

Nique had a tattoo of a skeleton plat formed heart with Jünior's name sketched through it, she had gotten it earlier today. Before the little homies turned around completely they got a full view of Nique's ass in that dress, jiggling freely with thunderous conviction. Nique was in full stride towards Nya who was looking good in her tight fitted blue True Religion jeans, orange True Religion tank top, and a pair of blue and orange Nike Air Max's, getting her thug on. Nique walked up to Nya just as she was approaching the trunk of her Lacrosse, gripping the book bag that Phenöm had dropped off extra tight in her left hand.

In her right hand was her S2 open to her text screen as she was texting back and forth with Jünior, he was home waiting for Nya to drop his money off. Nique stood off to the side watching Nya's every move, trying to figure out what her bestfriend was doing. Nya opened her trunk and quickly tossed the book bag inside before leaning inside reaching for her baby glock .22, which Jünior had given her.

Nique wanted so badly to ask Nya what the hell was in the book bag and what her and Jünior had been talking about so much lately, but she knew that Nya wasn't going to tell her a damn thing that Jünior was talking about. True, Nique was Nya's bestfriends and they told one another everything, but at the end of the day Nya's loyalty did and would forever remain with Jünior. So Nique knew that Nya would never tell her what was in the book bag, it was just some things that Nique new not to bring up. Nya stuffed her .22 inside of her black Juicy Couture bag as she closed the trunk, stepping towards the sidewalk where Nique was standing.

"Come on, Dom, your man told me to bring your ass home." Nya informed, smiling warmly.

"I know that his ass don't want nothing, probably getting tired of Ciara and Monique begging him to play doll babies with them." Nique laughed, as she reached for the passenger door handle.

"I don't know, he just asked me to bring your ass up the street."

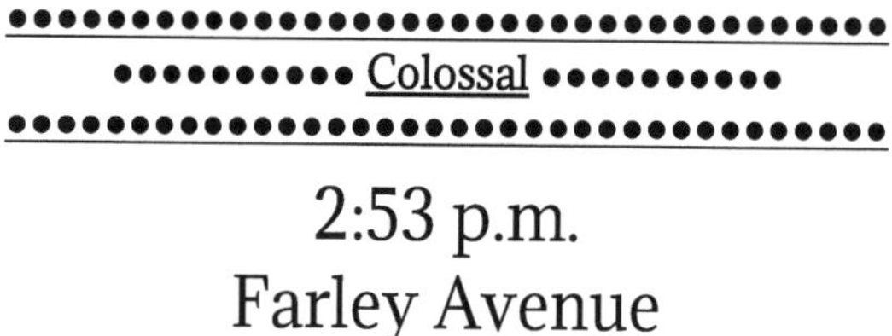

2:53 p.m.
Farley Avenue
■ Newark ■

"Allahu Akbar Allahu Akbar, Ash-Hadu An La Ilaha Ill-Allah, Ash-Hadu Anna Raheeman Rasul-Ullah, Haiya Ala Salat, Haiya Falat, Qumat Is Salat Qumat Is Salat, Allah Akbar Allah Akbar, La Ilaha Ill-Allah [*I bear witness that there is no deity besides God, who is without partner, And that Muhammad is His servant and messenger.*]." Phenöm chanted beautifully, standing atop his musalla.

Phenöm stood behind Jünior as he was up front standing on his musalla leading them into Maghrib salat, Mir stood to Phenöm's left and Chämp stood to his right. The four of them had just finished purifying themselves by performing Wudu, they each wore their Islamic garbs and their kufi's atop their heads proudly.

"Subhanaka Allahumma Wa Bihamdika Wa Tabaraka Ismuka Wa Ta A'ala Jadduka Wa La Ilaha Ghayruk [*Praise and glory is to, Allah, blessed is your name, exalted is your majesty and glory. There is no true, God, but you*]." Jünior firmly said, reciting the Du'aa-ul-istiftaah. Then, Jünior continued by chanting, "A'udhu Billahi Min Ash-shaytanir-rajim [*I seek the protection of, allah, against the accused satan*]..........Bismillahir Rahmanir Raheem, Alhamdu Lillahi Rabbil Alameen, Ar Rahmanir -----"

As Jünior began the Al-fatihah, Nya and Nique were downstairs getting out of Nya's Lacrosse, causing heads to turn in their direction. It only took Nya maybe 4 minutes to drive up the street to Jackie's house from Chadwick Avenue, being that close to the hood was always a plus for Jünior. Nya grabbed the book bag out of the trunk and proceeded towards the porch, with Nique right behind her. There were several bloods standing on the corner watching and lusting over the two of them, but they all knew who both Nya and Nique were.

Upon them reaching the second floor Nique went to knock on the door but Nya stopped her and pulled out her keys, she stuck them into the keyhole and twisted the knob. Nya had had a key to Jackie's apartment since Jackie had moved into the apartment, but Nique never really paid it any attention until now. Once again, Nya was Nique's girl but in Nique's mind she was getting tired of Nya and Jünior's quote/unquote brother/sister relationship, she was a woman at the end of the day and seeing another woman so close to her man was getting to her.

"Shenya, I didn't know that you had a key." Nique announced, as the two of them walked into the apartment.

"Girl, bye, I've had this key since I was they first moved in, Jünior ain't give you a key yet?"

"Yeah, right!"

"As much as you stay here and as lazy as everybody in here is, I'm shocked that you don't have one." she returned, turning around to lock the door back as Nique continued towards Jünior's bedroom.

Nique stormed into Jünior's room ready to lash out at Jünior but he was where she needed him to be, he wasn't there to accept her lashing. She looked over at the cable box and saw the time and knew exactly where Jünior was at, she had been with Jünior long enough to know what times of the day that Jünior offered salat. Nique was so aware of the prayer schedule that she would call Jünior and make sure that he was preparing to offer salat, just another reason that Jünior loved the ground that Nique walked on. The next thing that Nique noticed was Jünior had a bunch of newspapers spread out across the bed, accompanied by a book titled *Crime Pays* by Tha Twinz.

Nique had no idea why Jünior had all of those newspapers on the bed like that, but once he finished offering salat she was damn sure going to find out! Nya walked into the room and sat the book bag behind the door and then looked at the bed, she was also shocked at the way that his bed looked. In all of the years that she had been around Jünior she knew him to be a neat freak, this wasn't like him but she knew that he had to have had a good reason why his bed was like this. Nya gave Nique a hug and kiss her right cheek before spinning on her heels and leaving out of the room, leaving Nique there looking for answers. No sooner than Nya walked out of the room, Chämp and Mir came walking out of the closet with their musalla's in their hands.

"As salaamu alaikum, sis." Mir greeted, walking past her and heading straight out of the room without waiting for a response.

"Wa alaikum as salaam." Nique replied, giving the proper greeting back as Jünior had taught her.

"As salaamu alaikum, Nique." Chämp greeted, walking over to the bed and grabbing his iPhone and walking out of the room following Mir.

"Wa alaikum as salaam."

"As salaamu alaikum, bruh." Phenöm greeted lowly, as him and Jünior came strolling out of the closet.

"Wa alaikum as salaam wa rahmatullah." Jünior returned, as Phenöm gave Nique a hug and a kiss on her forehead.

"Hey, Johnnie."

"Make sure that you call my phone and let me know what's what." Jünior told Phenöm.

"I got you, skoob." Phenöm told him, releasing Nique.

"Nough said, make sure you lock the door on the way out."

"Bye, Johnnie."

"Never bye but always see you later, you say bye to a person that's dead." Phenöm replied, before leaving the room.

As soon as Phenöm walked out of the room Nique turned towards Jünior, and said, "Mustafa, there are some things that we need to discuss and I need you to keep it real funky with me."

"You know what, you're right, there are massive things that you and I need to talk about, however, let's start looking for a house in the meantime in between time." Jünior replied, patting the spot on his bed to his right where he wanted Nique to sit.

"H-h-hold on," Nique stuttered, closing her eyes and then opening them wider than they were before she closed them. "Boy, did you just say let's look for a house?"

"I mean we could always just stay on Chadwick Avenue in your apartment, or better yet we could just stay right in here with Jackie." he smiled.

"Jünior, don't fucking play with me like this, you wanna look for a house!" Nique exclaimed excitedly, forgetting everything that she was about to snap on Jünior about.

Picking up a piece of the newspaper that read Classifieds, Jünior simply replied, "Yes, a house."

"Oh, my fucking, God, I love you so much, I swear to, god, I love you so much!" she screamed excitedly, jumping into his arms nearly knocking him over.

"I love you, too."

"A house for just you and I?"

"No, a house for you, me, Ciara, Monique, and Mir."

"Oh, my, God, I love you!" Nique confessed, with tears in her eyes as she leaned in and gave Jünior a sloppy but very passionate kiss, then she pulled away and said, "I love you, I love you, I love you, oh, my, God, I fucking love your black ass sooooo much!"

"I love you, too," Jünior replied, grabbing Nique so that she could sit still long enough so that he look her in her eyes. "Will you move with me"

At that moment and time everything seem to just come to a nail pounding stand still from Nique, her heart rate quickly skyrocketed to a extreme rapid speed. Her mouth fell open with no remembrance of sound, her palms became possessed with sweat, her knees weakened ten times fold, and her head took on the weight of a feather as light as it was. Nique's throat quickly turned into a replica of a desert it was so dry. The Nile River couldn't compare to the flow of tears rivering down Nique's cheeks, there was so much emotion coming out of Nique right now. Never in a million years did Nique ever think that Jünior would come around to being her boyfriend, let alone buy her a house!

Sitting there on Jünior's lap somewhat shell shocked and nervous, all Nique could muster up was, "Bae, what did you do?!

"Huh?"

"What did you do, Mustafa, what did you do?" Nique asked, beginning to tremble uncontrollably.

"What did I do?"

"Don't play stupid, Jünior, what did you do that all of a sudden made you wanna marry me? Just days ago you wasn't sure if you even wanted to commit to me and move together and now you wanna buy me a house? What did you do? Tell me!"

"What did I do?"

"Yes, nigga.....what the fuck did you do!"

Wiping the tears from Nique's face trying not to ruin her MAC make-up before kissing her softly on her lips as he looked into her soul, Jünior told Nique, "I fell in love."

Nique felt like she was being re born all over again, and even though Jünior didn't come bearing a huge engagement ring, the way that Jünior had just confessed his souly love for her was more than any ring he could've gotten her. It was priceless!!! Nique pressed her lips against Jünior's as if they were the key to heaven, she knew that she could keep her lips like that forever. She leaned forward forcing Jünior's body back laying him flat, Nique lie atop of Jünior kissing him like she'd never kissed him before. Jünior had both of his hands gripping Nique's soft 42 inch ass while helping her dress rise to the occasion, as his dick became rock hard pressing against her stomach through the blue Levi jeans. Nique straddled Jünior after sliding her size 3 foot out of her Hermes sneakers, positioning herself atop his erection. Jünior slid hands over Nique's now exposed ass, pulling her g-string from between her ass cheeks, and gently slid his right index and middle fingers into Nique's drowningly wet pussy.

After Jünior took his fingers out of Nique's pussy and slid them into his mouth sucking her juices off, Nique kissed him deeply just to taste herself, before saying, "Yes, yes, baby, I will move with you!"

Tuesday May 4th, 2018

1:18 p.m.
High Street
▪ Newark ▪

"*There are 2 factors that influence the degree of difficulty in patience. First, is the degree of motivation when man wants to do something and secondly, how convenient is the intended action for man. If both factors exist, patience reaches it utmost difficulty and vice versa. While if one of the two factors disappear, it becomes difficult on one hand and considerably convenient on the other.*" the Iman delivered, as he stood before his community draped in his Muslim garbs. "*Thus, if man has no motive to kill, steal, drink wine, or commit atrocities, and these actions are inconvenient for him, then he is able to ward them off easily. Whereas a man whose desires are powerful and finds it convenient to act accordingly, then he hardly able to show constant perseverance. Hence, the ruler who abstains from injustice, the young man from indecency and the rich from worldly pleasures, command the highest status before, Allah [Suhhaanahu wa Ta'aala]. These categories rightly deserve, Allah's [Suhhaanahu wa Ta'aala], protection on the Day of Judgment so long as they bear hardships patiently. Therefore, the adulterous old man, the untruthful ruler and the haughty poor are severely punished because it would be more convenient for them to overcome such unlawful desires. Consequently, giving up patience in such situations sheds light on their insolence and rebellion* -----"

Jünior sat three rows back with Chämp to his left and Phenöm to his right, they were attending Islamic studies or Talim, which was the only thing that Jünior was able to leave the house for other than Jumah. They were down on High Street [Dr. Martin Luther King Jr. Boulevard] and W. Kinney Street at Rahman's Masjid, which was right next to Prince's chicken shack. Prince's used to be Utah's chicken shack back in the day, a chicken shack where you could get your head blown off while waiting on your order. The new Hill Manor was now up and people were residing within them, and the new Brick Towers was nearly complete.

The community was slowly getting back to the way it was before the city of Newark knocked down all of the buildings. They started with the Prince Street projects back in 2001. Jünior was happy to be out of the house but he was even more happy to be amongst his brothers and sisters of Islam, there was nothing that he cherished more than, Allah. Every time that Jünior came to Rahman's he learned something that he took with him in life, and with him living the way that he was living he needed, Allah, and his mercy. Jünior was all ears on what the Iman was talking about because patience was something that he was dealing with daily, with everything that he had on his plate, patience was highly needed.

Chämp was sitting there with his left arm in a sling after taking a bullet to the arm the night of the lick, shit had gotten real when they left out of the workhouse. The dudes from across the street had noticed Troy sitting in front of the workhouse too long, so they went and grabbed their guns to investigate, and that's when Doug, Phenöm, and Chämp came out of the workhouse. The three of them were each carrying bookbags on their backs, looking around suspiciously. And that's when the shots started ringing out. Phenöm dropped to the ground to check on Chämp and returned fire while Doug hopped into the Regal.

Phenöm firing back gave the crew the time that they needed to get in the car and make a getaway. Chämp had been pissed about getting shot and was really distant ever since it happened, he really blamed Jünior because Jünior knew damn well that he should have never been there in the first place. However, Chämp wasn't about to cry over spilled milk, what was done was done and there was nothing that either of them could do about it, he was alive and that's all that mattered in the end.

"*On the authority of Abu Hurairah, the Prophet [peace be upon him] said, 'Seven are those whom, Allah, will place under His protection on a Day when there will be no protection but His, namely: The just ruler, the young man who is brought up in worship of His Lord, a man whose heart is constantly attached to Mosques, two men who love one another for, Allah's sake, He alone brings them together and separates them, a man who, summoned by a beautiful woman, says: "I fear, Allah", a man who gives charity so much secretly that his left hand does not know not what his right hand had given, and a man who, remembering, Allah, in seclusion, and then sheds tears.*" the Iman continued, as he read from *The Way To Patience And Gratitude.* "*It requires constant perseverance to keep away from sins of the tongue and unchastity because their motives are powerful and easily accessible. Unfortunately, sins of the tongue provide delight for man, such as slander, telling lies, dispute, direct or indirect self-complacency, reporting people's utterances, deframing enemies and praising his votaries. On the authority of Mu'adh Ibn Jabal [may, Allah, be pleased with him] that the Prophet [peace be upon him] said*-----"

Jünior was amazed at what he was hearing, he loved to learn new things about the faith of Islam, he wanted to know as much about who he was as possible. Chämp sat there nodding his head up and down with a huge smile plastered across his face, Chämp was also learning new things about Islam that he didn't know. He was extremely intelligent but when it came to Islam he was still learning the basics, this was something that could keep his mind going until the death. Phenöm was deeply pulled in for the things that he was out in the streets doing, he needed, Allah, with him everywhere he went and he didn't miss a salat. Phenöm had many sins that he needed constantly wiped out, he knew that, Allah.

See, everything that he was doing out there in the streets. This was the only thing that Phenöm feared as he did do the evil shit that he did from time to time, Allah's, mercy was the only thing that Phenöm was concerned with. Jünior knew all about Phenöm's upbringing and he understood how Phenöm felt when it came to murder, it was a sense of art for Phenöm, his stress reliever. For the three young men sitting there listening they felt like each word was directed to them in one way or another, even the brother Tweek was in attendance sucking in as much as he could.

The Iman continued reading from *The Way To Patience And Gratitude*, stopping in between to explain certain things to the brothers. The Iman read and explained until it was time to offer Maghrib, the brothers came together and offered salat as a community. Once salat was finished the brothers started leaving out of the Masjid exchanging greetings and handshakes, Jünior was walking beside Tweek telling him about his latest troubles.

Tweek was dressed in a pair of dark blue JCME boot cut jeans, a black True Religion long sleeve T-shirt, a black Newark Brick City fitted, and a pair of black JCME Vasquez boots that resembled Gore Tex boots, he too was going through some legal problems which he was fighting. Jünior was alone in that category, the police knew how to come down on those trying to make a living for themselves and their family. Jünior was enjoying his night on the streets truly missing his freedom. Chämp had jumped into a cab and left because he had to pack so that he could get ready to go down to Millville and Camden, he needed to make sure that he didn't forget anything.

Phenöm on the other hand was right behind Jünior and Tweek walking a foot behind them with his desert eagle in the waistline of his blue True Religion jeans, covered by his white North Face thermal. The 3 of them walked towards Tweek's dark brown Oldsmobile Bonneville, behind his Bonneville was his little homies sitting inside of his rusted blood red Chevrolet Suburban with dark red limousine tinted windows. Jünior and Tweek had become close after spending much time at the Masjid together over the years, plus Tweek knew Fahim and respected his gangster. He'd known Jünior for years but they were both just into two different things, now Islam had brought them together in a positive way, bringing a group of brothers together instead of separating them.

"Man, I got mad shit going on right now, I got this dumbass case over my head which I'm on house arrest for," Jünior began, looking over at Tweek. "Then I gotta handle this other situation with Phenöm."

"What situation?" Tweek returned, giving Jünior a quizzed facial expression wondering what his young brother was going through.

"He might have a case that I'm tryna get him a lawyer for but the lawyer that I got is a waste of time."

"Look, give me your number and I'm goin' holla at me peoples and have him get in touch with you."

"Nah, it ain't that type of party, this case is grade "A" serious, we're talking life sentence serious." he informed, trying to explain to Tweek that Phenöm was looking at murder charges.

"Listen, he got my man Dope out of a life sentence after he was already sentenced to life without parole, when I tell you he's good, I mean just that!" Tweek replied, as two of his homies climbed out of the Suburban with guns in their hands.

"Aight, what are his prices like?"

"He's expensive but I'm goin' tell him to give you the best deal he can without cheating himself, I got love for y'all, plus I can't drain my brothers for a cause that's for the better."

"That's what's up, my number is [862] 555-3637, have him call me and I'll get him that money as soon as he can meet up with me." Jünior said, as Tweek climbed into his Bonneville sticking the key into the ignition.

"Trillz, I'ma do that as soon as I turn my phone back on, you said [862] 555-3637, right?"

"Yeah, good looking, Ahki."

"It ain't about nothing, as salaamu alaikum wa rahmatullah."

"Wa alaikum as salaam wa rahmatullah wa barrakatu." both Jünior and Phenöm returned, standing there feeling like they had just accomplished something.

Tweek pulled away from the curb, the Suburban filled with his little homies right behind him, Jünior turned to Phenöm, and told him, "I'ma handle this while you make that move, make sure that you hit my phone as soon as you touch down, and I'm goin' have Troy and Tàbi bring that to you."

"Aight, I got you."

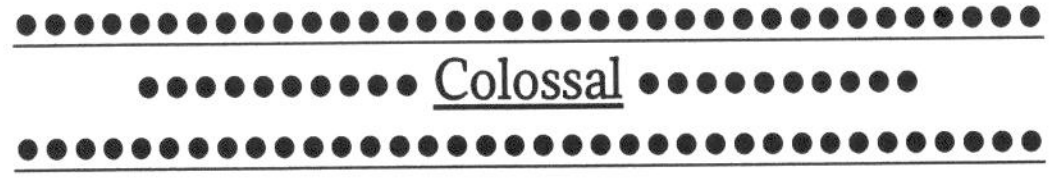

2:27 p.m.
Carl Miller Boulevard
▪ Camden, New Jersey ▪

"So what's the word?" Meer asked, sitting in the passenger seat of the rented Honda Civic that Chämp was in.

"Jünior, told me to come down and holla at you about moving some work that we got." Chämp replied, feeling uncomfortable with meeting with Meer.

"I don't know, what's the numbers looking like?"

"He said you would ask that."

"I would be stupid not to, so what's the numbers cause I'm doing good where I'm at." Meer shot back, looking out the window as Milla, Kayla, and Ma'Ma walked up to Mike and Ant.

"Aight, look, Jünior said that he was willing to beat any price that you're getting right now. He has a lot of work and he's confidant that you'll help him get rid of it."

"Well, let him know that I need time to finish what I have, but I told him I'll come through cause that's my guy. So you can tell the bull that I'll give him a holla when I'm done."

"Say no more, we'll be in touch." Chämp replied, as Meer grabbed the door handle and hopped out.

Chämp pulled off as Meer walked back to where he was standing with his crew. He knew that Jünior needed his help, nonetheless, Meer had a plug of his own that had been more than good to him, so crossing a diamond in the rough wasn't in Meer's DNA. Ant and Mike was standing there going back and forth about some chick that both were fucking, and the conversation was getting heated. Meer walked to his Jeep and sat in the passenger seat, and grabbed the bag of weed that was on the dashboard. Ma'Ma walked over and handed Meer a dutch to roll up with, cause she was trying to smoke on the arm. The conversation with Mike and Ant switched up to rap, and that's when Meer jumped in.

"Meek Mill can't fuck with the bull Cassidy." Mike admitted, leaning against the light pole that sat in front of Ma'Ma's house on Carl Miller Boulevard, just off of Pershing Street.

"Yeah, aight, the bull ain't fucking with Meek, I don't know how you can say that when Meek got way more money than bull." Meer replied, sitting in his passenger seat of his Cherokee with Milla standing in between his legs, rolling a blunt of sour diesel.

"Meer, everybody knows that Cassidy will murder the bull Meek on a track, and I fuck with Meek hard." Ant joined in, standing on the sidewalk with his arms wrapped around Kayla.

"Whatever, change the subject, bruh, I don't wanna hear that shit." Meer snapped, as his iPhone 3S started to vibrate on his hip.

"I don't know why you getting all mad for, neither one of y'all making shit for arguing over them niggas." Ma'Ma said, as Meer answered his iPhone after seeing that it was Y.G. calling him.

"I'm telling you!" Kayla assisted.

"Y.G., what up with you, bull?" Meer greeted, wrapping his left arm around Milla's waist after putting his phone on speaking so that he could finish rolling his blunt.

"Shit, just out here in my hood looking how I look, you heard?" Y.G. replied, sounding full of life as always. "I got these bitches out here choosing, you heard?"

"Fuck outta here, ain't nobody choosing yo ass."

"I wouldn't say that."

"I would," Meer laughed, just picturing his face as he said that, one of his signature statements. "What's good with you?"

"I'm in my hood chilling before I go back to the half, you heard, I only got three more weeks until I max out."

"Damn, bull, you should've been told me that you was out today, I would've drove up there."

"Nah, I'm supposed to be at work right now, but I said fuck it, I wanted to see how the hood was looking, you heard?" Y.G. shot back. "You know Clinton House is only like 45 minutes from New Brunswick, you feel me?"

"Meer, give me $10.00." Milla demanded, turning around to face him, giving him her best set of googly eyes.

"$10.00 for what?" Meer questioned, putting the finishing touches on the blunt that he was rolling, turning his head back towards the phone.

"I should slap the hell outta you, nigga, you down there holding out on me?" Y.G. asked, after hearing Milla's voice through the phone.

"Nah, this my young jawn, you can't have this one." Meer replied, still looking at Milla as she held her right hand out with her left hand on her hip.

"Just give me $20.00 because I said so!" Milla told him, stepping closer rubbing up against his dick print.

"Yo, let me call you back." Meer said, as a dark gray 2002 Grand Marquise pulled up on them double parking in front of Meer's Cherokee.

"Aight, make sure you get with me cause we need to chop it up, you heard?"

"I got you." Meer replied, before hanging the phone up and lighting the blunt.

"Ummm, hello!" Milla yelled, shaking her hand, as Meer hung up with Y.G. and sat his phone on the seat.

"How the fuck you go from $10.00 to $20.00 when I ain't even agree to the $10.00 in the first place?" Meer asked, noticing the two Caucasian men stepping onto the sidewalk in plain street clothes and police badges clipped to their waist.

"Shit!" Ant and Mike both gasped simultaneously, faces scrunching up disgustedly.

"Look what we have here," Dt. Jason Agholor commented, approaching Mike, dressed in a pair of black denim jeans, a black T-shirt, and a black Roc-A-Fella flight jacket over his bullet proof vest. “To what do we owe this surprise of a lifetime?”

“Don’t y’all got something better to do than to fuck with us!” Ma’Ma spat angrily.

“Shut the fuck up, bitch!” Dt. Paul Ertz spat, stepping closer to Meer and Milla with his hand on his holstered gun, dressed in a black Sean John sweatsuit, a black North Face shirt with his bullet proof vest underneath.

“Excuse you!” Ma’Ma screamed, staring at the cops with sheer disgust.

“Yo, you stepping way outta bounds, bull!” Meer barked, thinking about the black glock .40 that was sitting under his seat.

“Shut the fuck up, y’all little asses belong to me as long as y’all standing on our fucking block!” Dt. Agholor barked, turning around pointing his finger in Meer’s direction.

Meer was about to say something but the look on Dt. Agholor’s face told him a story worth being silent for, a look that he knew all too well! Meer’s heart dropped into the pit of his stomach as it felt like time had come to a stand stilling stop, he didn’t know where the shots were coming from but he knew that something was about to jump off. The human in him didn’t know whether to duck and have a chance at seeing the next day, whereas, the street in him craved to lean back and grab his .40 from under his seat and bust back. Dt. Ertz and Agholor both drew their guns aiming them in Meer’s direction with murderous intent, but clearly they weren’t aiming at him. Meer quickly shoved Milla to the ground before he laid across his seats, as Ant and Mike shoved Ma’Ma and Kayla to the ground just seconds before the shots rang out.

BOK, BOK, BOK, BOK, BOK, BOK, -----

"Oh, my God!" Kayla screamed in sheer terror, on the ground as glass shattered and rained down on her.

"You little fuckers!" Dt. Ertz yelled, as two bullets tore into his vest, pushing him feet violently.

BOC, BOC, BOC, BOC -----

"This some bullshit." Meer thought, lying across his seats.

BOK, BOK, BOK, BOK, BOK, BOK, BOK, BOK, BOK !!!

"Aaggghhhhh!" Dt. Agholor yelled, flipping off of his feet from three bullets that ripped into his vest accompanied by seven more.

SCCCUUUURRRRR !!!

••••••••••••••••••••••••••••••••••••••
•••••••••• Colossal ••••••••••
••••••••••••••••••••••••••••••••••••••

3:37 p.m.
Madison Avenue
▪ Newark ▪

"It seems like that shit is being spread out all over the city, everywhere I turn around motherfucka's is popping up with this dope stamped *Do Not Enter* and *Made In China.*" Boyn informed, sitting to Sul's left as they sat in the backseat of Sul's pitch black Chevrolet Trailblazer which was parked on Central Avenue and 9th Street.

"That means that the motherfucka that robbed us is out here somewhere selling that shit wholesale." Sul returned, nodding his head slowly as his son sat in the front seat watching *La Bamba*, a story about Ritchie Valens. "He's tryna get rid of it before I can track him down, we gotta find these motherfucka's before the family or Fahim gets wind of our lack of efforts. I need everything to stay casual until I finish setting things up, this shit can't fail."

"Fahim knows already, I talked to Cape the other day and he said that Fahim was pissed but said that he was giving you the benefit of the doubt."

"Shit, we gotta do more than what we're doing, it's good that you're out there putting it down so at least he knows our presence is in the streets, but we need the niggas responsible for this shit and we need them quick."

"I feel you."

"And find out who the fuck is giving Fahim information behind my back."

"I'm on that already cause I figured you didn't know anything about that." Boyn said, as a red Suburban pulled up beside them.

"Who the fuck is this?" Boyn asked, pulling out his .38 snub nose and cocking the hammer back, as Tupac's *Hail Mary* came booming from the confines of the Suburban with thunderous bass.

"Relax, that's my little bruh, Tweek, I told him to meet me here." Sul announced, stopping Boyn before he did something that would make their situation even worse.

Sul knew that Tweek rode around with goons with him that were always strapped down to the point of no return. Tweek had a lot to lose so he kept a car full of bloods with him. Not just that, Tweek tried to make sure that he had 1 or 2 cars filled with homies behind or in front of his car. He wasn't taking any chances in the streets that had claimed so many lives before him. When the back window of the Suburban came rolling down, Sul saw Tweek sitting there with a calm expression written on his face.

Tweek was wearing a white Paul George Indiana Pacers #13 jersey with the blue and yellow stripes going down the sides. He had his 2 youngest sons in the car with him sitting there watching *Tom and Jerry* on the flat screen TV that hung from the roof of the Suburban. They both were wearing Beats headphones which were attached to the TV. Sitting behind them in the 3rd row of the Suburban was Killa, and he was strapped with a P-90 Ruger hosting an extended clip.

"What's going on, Tweek, I almost thought you wasn't goin' come." Sul said, looking around to see how many cars Tweek had with him.

"Nah, I had to pick my boys up from their mother's house, you know how that goes."

"Yeah, I went through that this morning."

"What's up though, you got that for me?" Tweek asked, getting right down to business.

"Yeah but the numbers went up a little bit because of thi —"

"Hold up, wait, you gotta be kidding me, I'm not the nigga to pull this on, Su, my money always right and I always go hard." he replied, cutting Sul off before he could finish his statement.

"Yeah, you right, aight, look, have your people meet my people in about 10 minutes, you want the same order right?"

"Nah, double that shit, you out here wild'n and shit tryna over charge me, let me get a bigger order just in case you run into some problems again."

"Aight, I'm gonna need another 10 minutes to get it there, so make that 20 minutes tops."

"It don't matter, I got somebody over there already with all of the bread, just make sure that your people be there." Tweek said, before rolling his window back up and telling his driver to pull off.

"You must really fuck with that nigga, cause you charging everybody else more no matter what they buying." Boyn said, as the Suburban pulled off just as easily as it pulled up.

"Yeah, he just put in an order for a whole brick of dope, he usually gets 500 grams but now he wants a whole thing, I need that money." Sul returned, as a brown 2010 Dodge Ram 1500 pulled up right where Tweek's Suburban was double parked.

"Makes sense then."

"Rasul, my man, what's good, homie?" Ofc. Harvey greeted, after rolling his window down.

"Here, take that and keep it moving!" Boyn replied for Sul, after tossing $20,000.00 wrapped up in a brown paper bag into the window of the Ram 1500.

"Thank you, good doing business with you." Ofc. Harvey laughed, before pulling off.

"I can't stand them motherfuckas!" Boyn said, looking at the back windows of the Ram 1500.

"Yeah, me either, but they do what's needed of them." Sul told his little man.

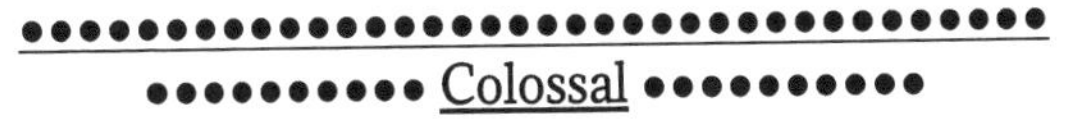

6:49 p.m.
Madison Avenue

'I shouldn't have left my babygirl a message/ saying I wouldn't be coming home/ cause I rather be alone/ she doesn't fully understand me/ cause I rather leave/ than achieve..........'

Donell Jones played softly throughout each of Nya's Lacrosse speakers as she made a left onto Madison Avenue, snapping her fingers to the high of *Where I Wanna Be*. The dudes on the corner of 18th Street and Avon Avenue standing in front of the old Mahogany's all the way down to Madison Avenue, were looking at Nya's Lacrosse knowing that it was her within.

This was the reason that Jünior had given Nya the money to tint her windows, he was overly protective over Nya as if they both shared the same womb. Each of them had tried their hand with Nya and had been shot down, Nya wasn't into dealing with dudes that were from her hood or around her family's house. Everybody in that area knew that the Lacrosse belonged to Nya because she was always parked on Madison Avenue, the young hustlers loved to see her pull up because they got to stare at her fat ass when she exited her car.

As Nya was pulling up in front of Jackie's house, Chämp was climbing out of his new but used money green 2003 Ford Taurus LS. There was no secret that Chämp had been in the worst of moods lately after getting shot, but since Jünior had blessed him with $6,000.00 he's been smiling a lot more. He was walking across the street as a brown 2002

Pontiac Grand Am rode down Madison Avenue playing Montell Jordan's *Get It On Tonight*, he started bobbing his head, mouthing the lyrics to the song.

Jünior had not only given Chämp $6,000.00 but he gave Phenöm and Doug $6,000.00, he ended up giving Troy $3,000.00 for her role in the lick. Jünior also gave Chämp a kilo of both coke and dope, a pound of weed, and 1,000 ecstasy pills, for him to do whatever he pleased.

Jünior put $7,000.00 towards Sofi's medical bills, he gave Rae and Tàbi a $1,000.00 for their pockets. Jünior also gave Nya money to put on Mona, Lissa, and Chelia's books. Jünior then gave Nya $20,000.00 which $10,000.00 of it was for herself. The other $10,000.00 was for his secured exit investment.

He gave Jackie $2,000.00, Mir $500.00, started bank accounts for Ciara and Monique, and gave Nya's mother, Brenda, $1,000.00. The two bank accounts that Jünior opened for his daughters were filled with $2,500.00, he was going to make sure that his babies were good regardless. He gave Brenda $4,000.00 for a down payment on him and Nique a house. There was no way that he was about to let Jackie sign for it, because she could be vindictive when not getting her way.

Jünior had never had $75,000.00 all at once but he knew that the next time that he got his hands on $75,000.00, he wasn't going to go through it in one day! After paying Lamina Robinson $5,000.00 to pick up his case along with Phenöm's case as well, then buying Nique a $3,000.00 engagement ring, he was broke all over again.

With his last $5,000.00 he gave Nique $3,500.00 for their dark red 2005 Chevrolet Tahoe, which left him with

$1,500.00. He put $1,000.00 to the side in his safe that he had Nya go out and buy for him. And then Jünior put the other $500.00 in his pockets.

Nya had double parked next to Jünior's Tahoe as Jünior, Jackie, Nique, Mir, Ciara, and Monique sat on the front porch, they had newspaper laid out while they ate crabs. Jünior and Mir were eating steamed shrimp. Jünior wasn't much of a crab eater because he didn't like having to go through so much for so little meat.

Chämp had walked up wearing a white Enyce button-up and a pair of True Religion jeans, with tan Timberlands on his feet. Nya climbed out of her Lacrosse in a green Gucci mini dress, and a pair of 6" Gucci stilettos. Nique sat on Jünior's lap wearing a pair of coochie cutting Levi's daisy dukes, a white short sleeve BeBe shirt, with a pair of white and black Jimmy Choo sneakers. Jünior was wearing a pair of multi-colored pajama pants, a black Galaxy T-shirt, and a pair of black on black Gore Tex boots. Monique and Ciara were dressed in matching pink Juicy Couture dresses, with Michael Kors sandals.

"As salaamu alaikum." Chämp greeted, walking up the steps.

"Wa alaikum as salaam." Jünior and Mir returned, while both sitting there peeling shells off of their shrimp before stuffing them into their mouths.

"Here." Nya said, walking up handing Jünior the signed lease and a set of keys to their new house. "Your godmother said thank you and everything is set, y'all could move in tonight if you wanted."

"That's good to hear." Jünior replied, nodding his head as 3 crack addicts walked past their house headed up to 18th Street to cop a hit.

"Jünior, let me holla at you in the hallway real quick." Chämp told him, standing there with his left arm in a sling.

"Aight, come on."

"Nya, look!" Nique beamed while standing up so that Jünior could get up, extending her left hand so that Nya could see her ring finger.

"Ooohhhh, girl, let me see!" Nya smiled, reaching for Nique's hand. "Bitch, this is beautiful, I'm sooo jealous right now! How many karats is it?"

"It's one, I don't really care about that though, as long as I marry my baby."

"So, what y'all goin' stay engaged until y'all turn 18?"

"Uh-uh, he's Muslim and within the religion of Islam we can marry at 16." she replied, smiling even harder about that information.

"Nique, you ain't no Muslim!"

"I don't have to be, as long as I am willing to follow him, that's all that matters. Which I am and will."

Inside of the hallway in the shadows of the dim lights that illuminated the walls, Jünior sat on the steps and looked at Chämp, and said, "What's good, bruh?"

"What's our next move, son?"

"I don't know your next move but I'm out to get mine, you know that already."

"So it's fuck me now, right?" Chämp asked, losing the smile that was on his face. "You blow up and forget about lil ole Chämp?"

"Fuck is you talking about! Do you have any idea how much shit I just gave you, nigga!" Jünior snapped, standing up with frustration written all over his face.

"What am I supposed to do?"

"What the fuck do you mean, you are supposed to get money, motherfucka!" he spat. "Look, you are my brother always, but I gotta do this on my own. When you finish moving what you got, come holla at me, I got prices that nobody can beat."

"You're right, I can do this." Chämp said, thinking that Jünior was going to be there to help him move his work. "Let's get money."

Peacing Chämp, Jünior pulled him into a hug, while saying, "That's right, nigga, let's get this fucking skrilla!"

TO BE CONTINUED

Dedicated to Myu & MemphMan
LONG LIVE THE GREATS

R.I.P.
to my aunt
Ronetta Rutledge
1969 - 2015

B.I.P.

TO MY GUYS

B.I.P. Tripple Beanz

Free Spaz aka S.O.
Free DiddyBop
Free 1090 aka
Da Governor
Free Rah Jigga

: ACKNOWLEDGEMENTS :

I want to give all praise to, Allah, the high and merciful, may peace and blessings be upon him. And to all of my brothers and sisters of Islam.

To my mother, Jackie, who has always been in my corner even when I wasn't in my own corner, I love you dearly, thank you for giving me life.

To my two Godmothers; Teniel, Michelle, and Samone, I love you all, thank you for loving me unconditionally.

A heartfelt R.I.P. to the following people; Joyce, Arnold, Linwood, Khalilah, Brenda, Jean, Ronette, Rafee, Keyon (*Kanye*), Raymond Faison Sr., Sadie Maye Brown, Tay Tay, Dale, Rock (*Malika's brother*), Hylenewn Qualls, Ruffin (*Flip*) Qualls, T-Man, Dena, Aunt Leola, Uncle Charles, Jeffery, J.D., Yameel, Fuzzy, Capo, Ernest (*Ern*) Bradley, Su, Ruger Rell, Weez, Bleep, Thomas (*T. Turn*) Turner, Millz, Hass a.k.a. Bishop a.k.a. Hard Body, Na, Lil Mikey, Fatal, Eric (*Uggie*) Bowens, Geda, Tripple Beanz, and all my other loved ones that are not here to witness this, keep watching over me.

To my aunts; Barbara, Michelle, Rasherra, Judy, Mattie, Jacinta, Ellen, Badia, Chrystal, Julie and Niecy Rutledge, and Joyce, thank you all for being there to care for me at different points within my life.

To my Uncles; Gary, Steven, Tony, Stanley, Gilbert, Yah Yah, Michael (*Ya Heard*), Musafa, Fateem, and Michael Wright, much love goes out to y'all.

To all of my sisters and brothers; Tahannah, Quetta, and Quadir Prince, Donte and Khashana Williams, Jazmin, CeCe Newton, Jamar Cotton, Semir, Gregory (*L.I.*) Baker; the love you've shown me over the years is surreal, Vernon Williams, and Chrystal Colbert I love y'all.

To my cousins; Sheila, Khalilah, Karen, Qiana, Spring, Abaya, Vito, Keisha, Kumar, ShaQuan, Shakeir, NaTasha, Mark Clark, Marcus, Nakita, Fee, Memph Man, Nay Nay, RaQuan, Terry, Sha Sha, Ra Banga, Cam, Flame Thrower, CK, Big Head, Adris and Andre Scott, Brittany and Russell Jenkins, Derrick, Darren, Aja, Quan, Kevin, Javon, Jakaii, Demetrius, L, Ibn (*730*) Gordon, Sharese, Lonzel, Na B.L., Brazy Boy, Bang Ru, Trisha, Ida, Sharod, Cookie, Dada, both Pookie's, Iiesha, Curtis (*Scootie*) and Connie Williams, Karrelle, Nucci Reyo, Jason Johnson and his brothers, and to the rest of my cousins that I didn't name, you know who you are, I love each and every one of y'all. Shout out to Mira, I can't forget you.

Screaming free my lil homie/brother; Rodney Williams aka Author Killa SOB.....

Free Author Killa SOB

THANK YOU SO MUCH FOR YOUR SUPPORT AND LOVE, I TRULY APPRECIATE YOU !!!!!

Please stay tuned for part 3, Condemned: *Havok's Havoc - a hostile takeover*

Malik D. Wilson

Made in the USA
Columbia, SC
21 September 2024

42129994R00107